BABY CAT-FACE

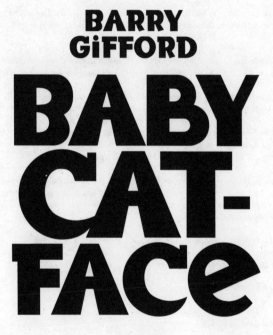

BARRY GIFFORD

BABY CAT-FACE

A NOVEL

Harcourt Brace & Company
New York   San Diego   London

Requests for permission to make copies of any part of the work should be mailed to:
Permissions Department, Harcourt Brace & Company, 6277 Sea Harbor Drive,
Orlando, Florida 32887-6777.

Portions of this novel, mostly in different form, appeared in the following magazines: First
Intensity (New York), The Double Dealer Redux (New Orleans), and Exquisite Corpse (Baton Rouge).

"Respect," by Otis Redding copyright © 1965 (Renewed) Irving Music, Inc. (BMI). All rights
reserved. Made in U.S.A. Used by permission of Warner Bros. Publications Inc., Miami, FL
33014.
"Honey Bee," written by Muddy Waters © 1959, 1984 Watertoons Music (BMI)/Administered
by BUG. All rights reserved. Used by permission.
Stamp design © 1960 United States Postal Service, all rights reserved.

Photograph credits, in order of appearance: photograph by Wanda Wulz, courtesy of
Alinari/Art Resource, New York; photograph by Stanley Stellar; photograph courtesy of
the Uwe Scheid Collection; photograph courtesy Reuters/Bettmann; photograph courtesy
of Quantity Postcards, San Francisco.

Library of Congress Cataloging-in-Publication Data
Gifford, Barry, 1946 –
    Baby cat-face: a novel/Barry Gifford. — 1st ed.
        p.   cm.
    ISBN 0-15-100183-9
    I. Title.
  PS3557.I283B33 1995
  813'.54—dc20 95-1148

Printed in the United States of America
First edition

A B C D E

Other Books by Barry Gifford

FICTION
Arise and Walk
Night People
The Sailor and Lula Novels:
   Wild at Heart
   Perdita Durango
   Sailor's Holiday
   Sultans of Africa
   Consuelo's Kiss
   Bad Day for the Leopard Man
A Good Man to Know
New Mysteries of Paris
Port Tropique
An Unfortunate Woman
Landscape with Traveler: The Pillow Book of Francis Reeves
A Boy's Novel

NONFICTION
A Day at the Races: The Education of a Racetracker
The Devil Thumbs a Ride & Other Unforgettable Films
The Neighborhood of Baseball
Saroyan: A Biography (with Lawrence Lee)
Jack's Book: An Oral Biography of Jack Kerouac
   (with Lawrence Lee)

POETRY
Ghosts No Horse Can Carry: Collected Poems 1967–1987
Giotto's Circle
Beautiful Phantoms: Selected Poems 1968–1980
Persimmons: Poems for Paintings
The Boy You Have Always Loved
Poems from Snail Hut
Horse hauling timber out of Hokkaido forest
Coyote Tantras
The Blood of the Parade

PLAYS
Hotel Room Trilogy

TRANSLATIONS
Selected Poems of Francis Jammes (with Bettina Dickie)

For my favorite boyzIImen—
Asa Colby, Kevin Nathaniel,
and Damon Doreado

Truth is not feasible, mankind doesn't deserve it.
—Sigmund Freud

The universe is queerer than we can suppose.
—J. B. S. Haldane

It's all the same to me, I'm already in paradise.
—Moro Dante Spada, a Corsican bandit,
upon being condemned to death

BABY CAT-FACE

BABY CAT-FACE

BABY AND JiMBO

"Take here dis lady in Detroit bludgeon her husban', chop up da body, den cook it. Talkin' 'bout payback! Whoa!"

"Baby, you oughtn't be readin' dem kinda lies is put inna newspaper. Ya know dat shit jus' invented, mannipilate y'all's min'. Make peoples crazy, so's dey buy stuff dey don't have no need fo'. Stimmilate da 'conomy."

"Wait up, Jimbo, dis gal got firs' prize. She skin him, boil da head, an' fry his hands in oil."

"What kinda oil? Corn oil? Olive oil?"

"Don't say. Lady be from Egyp', 'riginally. Twenny-fo' years ol'. Name Nazli Fike. Husban' name Ralph Fike. Police found his body parts inna garbage bag, waitin' be pick up. Whoa! Ol' Nazli was stylin'! Put onna red hat, red shoes an' red lipstick befo' spendin' hours choppin' on an' cookin' da body. Played Ornette Coleman records real loud while she's doin' it. Tol' police her ol' man put her onna street, shot dope in her arms, an' was rapin' her when she kill him in self-defense."

"Bitch was a hoojy, begin wit'."

"Jimbo, how you know? Plenty guys lookin' turn out dey ol' ladies."

"Was a hoojy."

"Aw, shit!"

"What?"

"She ate parts da body."

"Cannibal hoojy."

"Dis disgustin'."

"What else it say?"

"Can't read no more."

Jimbo Deal got up from the fake-leopard-skin-covered sofa and snatched the newspaper out of Baby Cat-Face's hands. He and Baby had been living together for six weeks now, since the day after the night they had met in Inez's Fais-Dodo, and he wasn't certain the arrangement was going to work out. She had a tendency to talk too much, engage him in conversation when he was not in a conversational mood. At thirty-four years old, Deal was used to maintaining his own speed. Since Baby Cat-Face, who was twenty-three, had come into his life, he had been forced to adjust.

"Woman ain' be clean fo' way back, Baby, you read da res'. Run numbers on guys since she come from Egyp', seven years ago. Car thef', drug bus', solicitin' minors fo' immoral purpose. A hoojy, like I claim. *Foreign* hoojy."

"Husban' put her up to it," said Baby. She lit a cigarette and stood looking out the window down on Martinique Alley. "She been abuse' as a chil', too."

"Dat's what dey all usin', now. Abuse dis, abuse dat. Shit. Says she be foun' sane an' sentence to life imprison. Shit. She prob'ly be queen da hive, have hoojies servin' on her in da joint. Big rep hoojy like her."

"Quit, Jimbo! Cut out dat 'hoojy' shit, all ri'? Tired hearin' it."

"Troof, is all. Since when you don't like to listen da troof?"

Baby sucked on an unfiltered Kool, then blew away a big ball of smoke.

"Swear, Mister Deal, you da mos' truth tellines' man in New Orleans."

Jimbo tossed the newspaper on the coffee table.

"I got to get ready fo' work," he said, and left the room.

Baby Cat-Face smoked and stared out the window. The sky was overcast. It was almost six o'clock in the evening and Baby was not sure what she was going to do while Jimbo pulled his night shift at the refinery in Chalmette. She saw two boys, both about twelve years old, one white, one black, run into the alley from off Rampart Street. They were moving fast, and as they ran, one of them dropped a lady's handbag.

"Baby!" Jimbo Deal shouted from the bathroom. "You gon' make my lunch?"

Baby took a deep drag of the Kool, then flicked the butt out the window into the alley. It landed, still burning, next to the purse.

"We got some dat lamb neck lef', darlin', ain' we?"

THE DWARF OF PRAGUE
AND THE DREADFULS

Baby Cat-Face had not used her real name, Esquerita Reyna, since her second, and last, year of high school. Even then, most of her friends and all of the members of her family called her Baby or Baby Cat-Face, as they had since she was born. She had been nicknamed Cat-Face for the most obvious reasons: she had green feline eyes and a tiny snub nose. Esquerita was the youngest of three sisters and two brothers born to DeDe Benavides and Refugio Reyna in New Orleans over a twelve-year period, and so she was dubbed Baby.

She attended St. Guerif of Rivages Grammar School, Turhan Bey Junior High, and St. Phoebe of Zagreb High School, all in N.O. It was during Baby's second year at St. Phoebe's, while on the class retreat, that Baby learned the legend of the Dwarf of Prague and the Dreadfuls. Sister Mercy Vermillion related the story of how in the fifteenth century A.D., a band of thugs and cutthroats called the Dreadfuls were terrorizing the good citizens of Prague. This group of murderous thieves specialized in kidnapping children of the rich and threatening to burn them alive unless their parents paid an enormous ransom. After the Dreadfuls had carried out this threat on two or three occasions, the families subsequently victimized quickly capitulated.

One day a gnomish dwarf named Desenfrenado appeared in Prague at the office of the mayor. Desenfrenado declared that he could rid the city of the Dreadfuls, but in return the citizens would have to build him a mansion behind the church in which he could live for the rest of his life, provide him with servants and funds adequate to a comfortable lifestyle, and allow him to go about the city naked during good weather. The mayor and most of his advisers were angered at the seeming effrontery of the dwarf, and were about to have him thrown into the street, when a member of the city council known as Raymond of Pest, a man who had come from the East and married a local woman, begged the mayor to indulge Desenfrenado. After all, said Raymond of Pest, there would be no harm in allowing the dwarf this opportunity to better himself, especially since the council had been unable to develop an effective plan of action. If the dwarf could eradicate the Dreadfuls, Raymond argued, Desenfrenado's request would be a small enough price to pay. The mayor and the other council members, having no immediate alternatives, thus sanctioned the dwarf's enterprise.

That night there was a full moon over Prague, and at ten o'clock Desenfrenado appeared nude in the town square. Mumbling to himself, the dwarf began to dance, gyrating wildly over the cobblestones around the deep well in the center of the square. Word of the dwarf's appearance spread throughout Prague, and soon most of its citizens were gathered in order to observe the event. Desenfrenado danced and danced, his movements becoming increasingly frenzied, his indecipherable mutterings growing louder, and—as Sister Mercy Vermillion delicately phrased it—his extreme maleness reaching a rather preposterous state. An hour or so into his mad romp, several of the audience, infected by the dwarf's dedication, themselves threw off their clothes and joined him in the dance. By midnight, virtually the entire population of Prague, including the mayor and his advisers, was whirling in intoxicated abandon around the dwarf.

Only nine men stood apart from the naked, swirling mass. Suddenly, the dwarf bolted from among the throng and began to run in a circle around the isolated men, shouting, "These are they! These are they!" The citizens turned their attention to the nine nonparticipants and advanced on them, mumbling and drooling as they came. The nine men, quickly surrounded, could not escape. They fell to their knees and begged forgiveness for their sins, confessing that they were indeed the Dreadfuls who had kidnapped and burned the children. No sooner had these words escaped their mouths than the furious crowd tore the men's limbs from their bodies, their tongues from their heads, and crushed their skulls on the cobblestones.

Desenfrenado was provided with his mansion and supported thereafter by the citizens of Prague. When in fair weather he chose to go about the streets of the city unclothed, the citizens greeted him as affectionately and respectfully as they did when he was clad. The dwarf, Sister Mercy Vermillion told her class, lived to be very old. Desenfrenado had not been accorded sainthood, she explained, due to his own choosing. Before he died, Desenfrenado declared that he wanted forever to remain a humble man, as ordinary in memory as he had been in life. Remember, he said on his deathbed, it is always the most dreadful among us who ultimately are revealed to be the most timid.

Baby Cat-Face never forgot the story of the Dwarf of Prague. She had told it to every man she had slept with more than once, all of whom, with the exception of Jimbo Deal, had said that it was the most ridiculous story he had ever heard. Jimbo had only nodded and said, "Baby, funny, ain't it, how there never be a dwarf around when you need one."

Jimbo, Baby hoped, would turn out to be the kind of man who never lost his sense of humor.

RAT TANGO

" 'What you want, baby I got it. What you want, baby I got it.' "

"Say, what?" Baby Cat-Face said to the red-haired, café au lait woman who was singing and dancing the skate next to the jukebox, her back to Baby.

"Huh?" the woman said, doing an about-face, keeping her skates on. "How come there ain't mo' Aretha on this box? 'R-e-s-p-e-c-t, find out what it mean to me,' " she sang-shouted, beginning to swim and shimmy. "Sock-it-to-me sock-it-to-me sock-it-to-me!"

The woman wiggled and shook, causing Baby and another patron of the Evening in Seville Bar on Lesseps Street to grin and clap.

"Down to it, Radish!" shouted a fat man standing next to the pay phone. He banged his huge right fist on the top of the black metal box. "Be on time! Ooh-ooh-ooh!"

The dancing woman looked at Baby, and asked, "You say somethin'?"

"Thought you was talkin' to me, was all," said Baby. "You say 'baby.' "

"Yeah, so?"

"That's my name, Baby."

The woman smiled, displaying several gold teeth, one with a red skull painted on it. "Oh, yeah? Well, hello, Baby. I'm Radish Jones. Over here playin' the telephone's my partner, ETA Cato."

The fat man nodded. He was wearing a porkpie hat with a single bell on the top with DALLAS printed on a band around the front of it, and a black silk shirt unbuttoned to the beltline, exposing his bloated, hairy belly.

"Happenin', lady?" he said.

"ETA?" said Baby.

Radish laughed. "Estimated time of arrival. Cato's firs' wife name him, 'count of his careless way 'bout punctchality. Come we ain't seen you in here before, Baby?"

"Firs' time I been, Radish. My ol' man, Jimbo Deal, tol' me check it out."

"Shit, you hang wit' Jimbo? Shit, we know da man, know him well. Don't we, Cato?"

"Who dat?"

"Jimbo, da oil man."

Cato nodded. "Um-hum. Drink Crown Royal an' milk when he up, gin when he down."

"Dat him," said Baby.

"Where he at tonight?" Radish asked.

"Workin'."

"Well, glad you come by, Baby. We front you a welcome by."

"Rum an' orange juice be nice."

"Say, Eddie Floyd Garcia," Radish called to the bartender, "lady need a rum an' OJ."

The bartender mixed Mount Gay with Tang and water and set it up for Baby.

"Thanks, Eddie Floyd," said Radish. "This here's Baby."

"Hi, Baby," the bartender said. "Round here we call dis drink a Rat Tango, as in 'I don't need no rat do no tango at my funeral.'"

Eddie Floyd Garcia, a short, wide, dark blue man of about fifty, winked his mist-covered right eye at Baby. Up close, she could see the thick cataract that covered it.

ETA Cato traded off dancing with Radish and Baby to the juke over the next couple or three hours, during which time they consumed liquor at a steady clip, Eddie Floyd making sure to keep their drinks fresh. It was a slow night in the Evening in Seville. Other than a few quick-time shot and beer customers, the trio and Eddie Floyd had the place to themselves. Baby learned that Cato worked as a longshoreman on Celeste Street Wharf, and Radish did a thriving nail-and-polish business out of her house on the corner of Touro and Duels called The Flashy Fingers Salon de Beauté.

Sometime past two A.M., Radish decided that ETA Cato had danced one too many times in a row with Baby Cat-Face. Johnny Adams, "The Tan Canary," was seriously wailing "I Solemnly Promise" when Radish flashed a razor under Cato's right ear, cutting him badly.

"Damn, woman!" Cato yelled. "What you do that for?!"

Radish Jones shook a Kool from a pack on the bar, stuck it in her mouth, but couldn't quite hold her lighter hand steady enough to fire up the cigarette.

Eddie Floyd Garcia grabbed a rag, vaulted over the counter, and knelt next to ETA Cato, who had slid to the floor, holding his right hand over the cut. Blood was jumping out of his neck.

"King Jesus! King Jesus!" screamed Baby, backing away.

Eddie Floyd applied pressure to Cato's wound with the rag, but the bleeding did not abate.

"Call a ambulance!" Eddie Floyd cried. "Look like a artery be sever'."

Radish did not pay any attention to Cato's predicament, absorbed as she was in her attempt to torch the Kool. Baby grabbed the phone and dialed 911. When a voice answered, she started to talk, then stopped when she realized it was a recorded message requesting that the caller please be patient and hold the line until an operator became available.

Baby forced herself to look at Cato. He coughed, lurched forward, and fell back against Eddie Floyd. Cato turned toward Baby and opened his eyes wide. She thought he was going to say something, but he died with his mouth half open, staring at her. A human being came on the line and asked Baby, "Is this an emergency?"

ONLY THE DESPERATE
DESERVE GOD

"In Yuba City, California, two severed hands were found in a K-mart shopping cart. The grisly discovery was made at about four P.M. Sunday by a clerk collecting carts, a Yuba City police spokesman said. The hands are being treated as evidence in a crime, but it will take a forensics expert to determine for sure that the body parts found are, in fact, human and whether homicide is indicated."

"There just ain't no end to human mis'ry," Baby said out loud to herself, as she switched off the radio next to her and Jimbo's bed.

Baby Cat-Face had spent most of the previous three days drifting in and out of sleep, depressed by thoughts of the incident she had witnessed in the Evening in Seville Bar. After Radish Jones slit the throat of her boyfriend, ETA Cato, who expired on the barroom floor, flooded by his own blood, Baby had gone stone-cold with shock. Jimbo Deal told Baby later that the police had brought her home and that he had put her to bed after feeding her the Valium mints the NOPD nurse had safety-pinned in a tiny plastic bag to Baby's blouse.

She had eaten sparingly during this time, only Rice Krispies and dry toast with tea. Jimbo had stayed home from work for two days, "Baby-sittin'," as he called it; but today he had had to go, afraid that he would be fired if he did not. Jimbo placed a loaded Ruger Bearcat in Baby's bedside drawer and told her to protect herself with it if she had to until he came home.

Baby reached over with her right hand and switched the radio back on, tuning it until she found an interesting voice, and left it there.

"People, when I say you got to *stand up* to God, I mean you got to *challenge* his word!" said the voice. "You got to be *bold* enough for Him to pay you any mind. Only the *desperate* deserve God, don't you know? Hallelujah! Are you *desperate* yet? Are you *ashamed* yet? Are you *frightened* next to death yet? Well, well, well—you *should* be! Yes, you should, you should! This is the *time*, people, the *only* time you got to hear God's word. It don't matter what your name is, what color you are, what *size* or financial condition, no! You got to *stand up* to him right now or it's snake eyes for the planet! Yeah, we got to do this little thing together, people, make it work *right*. Get our neighbor to *admit* how desperate he or she is so we can get *on* with this holy war, 'cause that's what it is, a *holy* war! Standin' up to God means standin' up to the beast in the street, the one soon's spit poison in your eyes as look at you. You *got* to know what I'm talkin' about, people, or *die stupid!*"

"I know," Baby said. "I know what you sayin'."

"All *right*, then!" said the voice from the radio. "*Stand up to*

God! Do what's necessary! Most of you desperate and don't know it!''

Baby turned off the radio. She heard the front door to the apartment open and then quietly close.

"Jimbo? Honey, that you home already?"

A short person wearing a red ski mask stepped into the bedroom. The intruder held a .45 automatic pistol with both black-gloved hands and pointed it at Baby. Baby threw a pillow at the gun and rolled off the bed onto the floor, pulling down the bedside table as she fell. She grabbed Jimbo's Ruger from the drawer, swung it toward the intruder, closed her eyes, and pulled the trigger twice. Baby opened her eyes and saw that she was alone in the room. She held the Bearcat straight out in front of her as she got to her feet.

"Come on, muthafuck!" Baby yelled. "I stand up to God now!"

Baby crept stealthily from the bedroom into the living room. The front door was closed. The kitchen, which was in full view from the living room, was empty. The only other place a person could be hiding was the bathroom.

"Come out of there!" Baby shouted, pointing the Ruger at the closed bathroom door. "Or sure as shit I gon' bust a cap up yo' butt!"

There was no sound from the bathroom, so Baby Cat-Face fired two rounds through the door. She kicked it open and charged inside, firing two more shots into the shower stall.

Baby looked around: there was nobody but her in the bathroom. She saw her reflection in the mirror above the washbasin. Her eyes were slashes of red on her face.

"King Jesus," she said, "am I hallucinatin'?"

A police siren wailed and Baby heard a car screech to a stop in Martinique Alley. She sat down on the toilet seat and let the handgun drop to the floor.

"Maybe I be *too* desperate," said Baby.

BiRDS OF THE eVeNiNG

Dear Jimbo Sweethart.
I pretty much had it with NO so am decide to visit my Aunt
Graciela in Carolina for a spel. The violent got to me lover but I
get strong an be back soon. Needin some peecefull time to collec
my thots.
  Love
  Baby XXOO

Baby Cat-Face taped the note to the refrigerator door, knowing that as soon as Jimbo Deal got in from work he would
open it to take a cold beer. She picked up her ersatz ocelot
suitcase, left the apartment, and walked the two and a half
blocks to the Southern Trails bus terminal on the corner of
Feliciana and St. Claude. Baby bought a round-trip ticket to
Corinth, North Carolina, a mountain town four miles north-
west of Asheville, and sat down in the waiting room. The
evening bus to the East Coast was scheduled to leave in twenty
minutes.

"Y'all look like a bird, darlin', a bright-colored bird flyin'
the coop. Is you?"

Baby looked at the person who had spoken, a woman seated

to Baby's left. She was about forty, Baby guessed; a good-looking, sepia-skinned lady. The woman was wearing a black half Stetson hat with a pearl-headed stickpin in the brim.

" 'Scuse me?" said Baby.

"Nothin' worth excusin', honey," the woman said, and laughed hoarsely. "Just wondered if you was needin' comp'ny. Happens I prefer it."

"My name's Esquerita Reyna, but ever'body call me Baby."

The woman extended her right hand, three fingers of which were adorned by multicolored stone rings, and replied, "Hello, Baby, I'm Claudette Crooks, but everyone knows me as Sugar."

Baby shook hands, then jumped in her seat.

"Don't tell me you *Sugargirl* Crooks?! The singer? One who done 'Melt Me to the Bone' and 'Dude Don't Get Much Rest When He Be Sleepin' Around'?"

"That was me, all right. Days gone by."

"You were my favorite singer when I was at Turhan Bey Junior High School on Tonti Street! Can't believe it's you!"

"Yass, girl, it's me. Now a ol' lady waitin' on the bus."

"Shit, Sugar, you ain' ol'! Why, you one of the all-time greats!"

Sugar smiled and took Baby's hands in hers.

"Thank you, Baby, you make me feel good. Truth is, I been all through with that mess a long time. Only singin' I do now is at church. Where you headed, child?"

"Corinth, North Carolina, see my aunt. Get away from New Orleans awhile."

"Ain't that good! We practic'ly neighbors, bein' I'm bound for Asheville, few miles down the road."

"You live there or here?"

"I quit city life soon after I quit the recordin' business. Been in New Orleans to attend the funeral of one of my cousins, CeCe Dobard, died of breast cancer, Lord have mercy."

"Sorry to hear that."

"Uh-huh. CeCe was a sweet gal. Only forty-two, a year older'n me. The Lord callin' us in no particular order, it look like. A woman need to be ready."

"Why you quit makin' records, Sugar? I never could get enough of you as it was."

"Bless you, Baby, fo' sayin' that. It's a old, tired story been told too many times. Jus' say a man in the middle of it."

"Tore you down, huh?"

"Sister, the minute a woman allow a man take responsibility for her life, she fixin' to let him ruin it."

The boarding call for the East Coast bus came over the loud-speaker and Sugargirl Crooks rose abruptly to her feet.

"Come on, Baby," she said, "we need to get us a seat together close by the toilet. My kidneys don't take kindly to the road."

UNTAMED

Sailor Ripley pressed his right foot against the accelerator pedal of the ochre 1958 Buick Limited he'd just bought while holding his left foot down on the brake pedal until the acrid odor of aggravated rubber singed his nostrils, then expertly lifted off the brake precisely as his right big toe hit metal, laying a fifteen-foot strip of Firestone's finest in front of Alabama Billy Caldwell's Car and Major Appliance Lot. Sailor tore out Fayette Street and swung a hard right onto Hatteras Boulevard, headed for Federal Highway. He had turned eighteen years old the day before and today had paid three hundred dollars cash money for the machine of his dreams.

For two months, Sailor had begged Billy Caldwell not to sell the Banana Monster, as Sailor's sixteen-year-old girlfriend, Lula Pace Fortune, called it, to anybody but him. Sailor promised Billy he would have the three hundred in hand by the first of May; he had, and now the car was his. Robbing Chigger's Chicken Cottage in Bolivia had not been on the original agenda, of course, but Sailor couldn't count on Caldwell's keeping the Buick after the first, so Chigger's became fair game. Sailor did not consider himself an habitual criminal. Penny-ante stickups, he reasoned, could not be classified as heavy-duty crimes any more than copping a blow job from a strange girl could be considered cheating on your girlfriend. "Blow jobs ain't sex," his daddy used to say. "It's just a little somethin' brighten up the day." Sailor had no trouble putting stickups in the same category.

When he pulled up in front of Bay St. Clement High School, Lula was waiting for him. She shrieked when she saw the yellow Limited, threw her books into the backseat through the open passenger-side window, and climbed in.

"Sailor," Lula cried, her long black ponytail flipping as she swiveled her head, inspecting the vehicle, "this short is the most!"

He grinned, took an unfiltered Camel from behind his left ear, put it between his lips, deftly manipulated a match with his right hand without removing it from the matchbook, and lit the cigarette.

Sailor expelled a blue ribbon of smoke and said, "Hoped to please you, peanut. Purpose of my life, in fact."

Lula threw her arms around Sailor's neck and squeezed him to her, pressing her practically brand-new breasts against his black cotton Fruit of the Loom T-shirt.

"Oh, Sail," she sighed, "no matter what my mama says, you're the one, you know?"

Lula stroked the brilliantined-back wing of blue-black hair on the left side of Sailor's head with her right hand.

"I know," he said.

"I mean not only in the entire state of North Carolina, but in the whole civilized world."

Sailor laughed and tossed the Camel out the window.

"How 'bout the uncivilized part?"

"Need to know more about it before reachin' a conclusion," Lula said, and giggled. "So far, though, you're the most uncivilized person I've ever had anythin' of a serious-type nature to do with."

"You figure I'm uncivilized, huh?"

She reared back her head and looked at him.

"I guess untamed is more like what I'm gettin' at. Yeah, Sailor, y'all definitely are the untamed type."

He clutched her slender but sturdy body to his, kissed her gently on the mouth, and said, "You fixin' to tame me, then, Lula? Make me do right by you?"

"Hell, baby," said Lula, gently raking the fingernails of her right hand across his chest, "the more wrong you do with me, the more right it feels."

Lula kissed Sailor as deeply as she could, and suddenly felt her entire body become liquid. Students walking by the car peeked in and laughed and made sordid comments but neither Sailor nor Lula paid them any mind.

"No matter what, Lula," Sailor said, looking into her deep gray eyes, "no matter what happens ever anywhere, we got it perfect right this very untamed moment. No way nothin' or nobody can ruin it. Not even Mrs. Marietta Fortune."

"Sailor Ripley, you're the most romantic boy? I may be only sixteen years old but that don't mean I don't know just how lucky I am."

"Tell you, Lula, I ain't the smartest person on the planet, but I got a feelin' this kinda luck don't never run out."

TRUE BELIEVERS

"What say we go on a run this weekend, Lula?" Sailor said, as he and his sweetheart cruised in the Limited along the Cape Fear Turnpike.

Sailor kept the Buick at an even fifty. All four windows were down, allowing the fragrant early May air to circulate inside the car.

"This is some kinda dreamy ride, Sail," said Lula, "you know? Just breezin' like this?" She closed her eyes.

Sailor shook loose a Camel from a pack on the dash, stuck it between his lips, and punched in the lighter.

"Ever'thin' works," he said.

Ten seconds later, the lighter popped up and Sailor pulled it out and lit his cigarette. He replaced the lighter with his right hand, which he then inserted between Lula's thighs.

"Feelin' naughty, huh?" she said, spreading her legs a bit.

"You bet, darlin'. What you think about what I said? We can be almost anywhere in a couple hours."

"Gray an' yella go good together, don't they, Sail?"

"Sure, peanut. Why you ask?"

"Color my eyes an' color the car. Really suits me."

Sailor took the Camel out of his mouth with his left hand,

flicked the ash out the window, stuck the cigarette back on his lower lip and grabbed the steering wheel. The fingers of his right hand remained mashed between Lula's legs.

"Perfec' Friday afternoon like this," he said, "ought to be we're goin' somewhere special."

"Like New Orleans," said Lula. "I been waitin' to go back there since I was eleven an' visited the city with my mama and daddy. We stayed in a big hotel had the most gigantic ceilin' fans I ever seen in the dinin' room. I recall our havin' to walk past about thirty tattoo parlors, though, to get to the river. Never have seen so many tattooed men in my life. Mama said they's mostly gone now, the city bein' cleaned up, which is too bad, I think. Trashy parts of a city is always the most interestin' parts."

"Take us a couple days to get there, honey. No way I could get you back for school on Monday."

"Oh, I know, Sailor. I just been thinkin' 'bout N.O. lately."

"We'll go there someday, Lula, I promise. Meantime, what say we head for Corinth, that little town in the mountains I told you about? Your mama ain't gonna be back 'til Sunday night, right? We get home before then."

"Yeah. She an' Auntie Dal drove to Charlotte this mornin' to see my daddy's ol' friend and business associate Mr. Santos, man who paid for Daddy's funeral."

"He the one send flowers to your house all the time?"

"To Mama, every Thursday. Think he been sweet on her since before she married Daddy."

"So, we goin' to the mountains?"

"Mama be callin' the house, see I'm there."

"She get back, tell her you was stayin' with a girlfriend."

"Guess I could call Patsy Strangelove, have her back me up I tell Mama I been at her house. Her daddy's dead, too, and her mama ain't hardly ever around, wouldn't know if I been there or not."

"Sure, peanut. You call Patsy soon as we get to Corinth. I know a cool place we can stay at just outside town, called the South China Sea Motel."

"Funny name for a motel in the mountains of North Carolina."

"Guy who owns it used to be in the navy. Been ever'where, 'cludin' China, I guess."

"How you know this place, Sailor? You take other girls there?"

Lula opened her eyes and pushed his hand away.

Sailor laughed and said, "No, darlin', I just heard about it, is all. Buddy of mine named Taylor Head goes up once a month or so, stays at the South China Sea."

"What for?"

"Keeps his collection of Kim Novak photos there. Mostly ones of her in Picnic and The Man with the Golden Arm. Has maybe a hundred of 'em."

"Why? An' why's he keep 'em there?"

"Likes Kim Novak, I guess. Way she looked in them old movies. Don't really know why he stores 'em at the motel, 'cept maybe for safekeepin'. Could be Taylor'll be there this weekend and you can check out the photos yourself."

"Can think of better things to do, baby," Lula said as she took Sailor's right hand and replaced it between her legs.

He grinned and kicked the Buick past sixty. To be eighteen years old zooming along in a terrific car with an almost perfect girlfriend who can't hardly get enough of you on a breezy spring afternoon in the South was just about it, thought Sailor Ripley. Whatever lay ahead, he allowed, might turn up something even better, but this was enough for now, and he was glad as hell he had the good sense to realize it.

"Sail?"

"Uh-huh?"

"Gotta be somethin' not entirely unweird 'bout a boy keep all them pictures of a old actress like that."

"Peanut, might be it's all he got, you know?"

"Mean, he ain't so lucky as us."

"Not by half, honey. Might could be nobody is."

Lula closed her eyes again and listened to the wind in her ears.

"Young and innocent as I am," she said, "I do believe I know the truth when I hear it."

At seventy-five miles per hour, the Buick began to shimmy.

TiGHT FiT

"When the world is zoomin' by, like out the window of this bus," Sugargirl said to Baby, who sat to Sugar's right, next to the aisle, "could be we're watchin' time pass. Mean, it won't never be the same, completely the same. Not so long as the Lord keep pushin' the way he do."

"Pushin'?"

"Yeah. Ain't you noticed how he don't let nothin' or nobody *be* more'n seconds at a time? Not even seconds, really, you think about it."

"Prob'ly why there ain't any lastin' peace 'til a body die," said Baby Cat-Face, "an' even then, worms is on it."

"The body bein' picked at but the soul be free."

The bus was about twenty-five minutes outside of Corinth, North Carolina, when a very large, pear-shaped, tan-faced woman wearing a ratty yellow wig walked up the aisle from where she had been sitting in the rear to the front of the bus and stood next to the driver. Cradled across her heavy bosom was an AK-47 assault rifle.

"Word up!" the woman announced. "I ain' jokin' an' I don' be dopin'. My name is Daylight DuRapeau. My mama say she name me Daylight 'cause she had a feelin' the world was gonna see a whole lotta me. And as y'all can positively witness, there be considerable of me to see.

"I speck mos' y'all gon' be disappointed to learn we makin' a detour here, the driver don' mind. An' he don't. Not while I holdin' an automatic instrument the only point to ownin' is causin' all kinds calamity an' destruction. Up ahead here, driver, we gon' come to a turn-off for the one ninety-one highway. You know it?"

"Uh-huh," said the driver, not taking his eyes off the road.

"Good," Daylight said. "You follow that along the French Broad River 'bout sixteen miles to Tight Fit, town wedged in between the river and side of a mountain. I let you know what to do nex' we get there."

"This world get more uncertain by the hour," Sugargirl said.

"Should never lef'," said Baby.

"Truly folks," said Daylight DuRapeau, "don't mean to make y'all nervous. Fack, this might could turn out to be an entire enjoyable experience fo' all us involve, volunteer or not."

"Somethin' 'specially strange 'bout dis woman," whispered Baby. "Look in her eyes what my man Jimbo call like a deer in da headlight."

Sugargirl Crooks closed her eyes and prayed silently. Baby

Cat-Face sat stone-still, feeling nothing except for the twin trickles of perspiration emanating from her armpits.

"Oh let the wickedness of the wicked come to an end," said Sugar, "but establish the just; for the righteous God trieth our hearts."

THE BIG KISS

"Sail on, sail on, my little honeybee, sail on," Muddy Waters sang. Sailor and Lula danced close, inching across the worn brown carpet in room six of the South China Sea Motel, lights off with the radio loud enough to cover up truck noises from the highway.

"Peanut," Sailor Ripley whispered, "my dick is thick as a brick."

Lula laughed and held her man tight. "I know, darlin'," she said, "it's cuttin' into my belly like a butcher knife. Just let's dance some more, though, before we go to doin' it, okay? I'm feelin' real dreamy right at the minute."

"Sure, baby," said Sailor. "I won't have no trouble keepin' the thought."

There was a loud thump against the west wall of Sailor and Lula's room, as if someone had thrown a chair against it. Sailor and Lula stopped dancing and waited for voices, but they heard none. They gripped each other again and had just pushed together when another thump exploded against the wall.

"What you think, Sail?"

"Guess I better go see."

"Careful, darlin'."

"You bet, peanut. Stay inside."

Sailor opened the door to their room, poked out his head, and looked around. Except for up on the highway, nothing was moving. He stepped outside, walked down to room five, and put his left ear to the door. Just as he did, another loud sound issued from the interior. Sailor knocked hard.

"Y'all all right in there?" he shouted.

There was no answer, so Sailor knocked again.

"Y'all need some help?"

The door opened, revealing a very short Hispanic man about thirty years old. Long, black, uncombed hair fell over his face; he wore a dirty white T-shirt, stained brown trousers, no shoes or socks. He needed a shave but had no mustache. His black eyes were glazed over; he looked stunned, as if he had just been hit in the head.

"What?" said the man. "What you're sayin'?"

"We heard them loud sounds, thumps on the wall. We got the room next door. Thought maybe there was some kinda trouble."

"No, no troubles. I was asleeping."

"Think maybe you mighta been kickin' the wall in your sleep, then."

"Si, si. Sometimes I have big sueños, very powerful."

"Sueños. Them's dreams, right?"

"Dreams, si. Sorry I am disturbin' you."

The man held out his right hand.

"*Me llamo Pepe Pescuezo*. From Murgatroyd, Tejas."

Sailor shook hands with him.

"Sailor Ripley, from Bay St. Clement, North Carolina. You a long ways from Texas, Señor Pescuezo."

"This a holy place, man. Ain't that why you here? You with your wife?"

"Uh, yeah. Me and her just drove over for a couple days. What you mean a holy place?"

"Oh, man, this is Corinth, right?"

"Corinth, yeah. Corinth, North Carolina."

"Well, you know this the place all the big-time changes gonna come down, anytime soon. You stick around to see 'em, man. Happen soon, really soon."

"Didn't hear nothin' about nothin' 'bout to happen here."

"This is the place Pablo the Apostle wrote about, man, you know. Where all the evil shit was goin' down. The wickedest place on earth. He wrote a letter to the Romans about it."

"How you know this?"

"Shit, man, it's in the Bible. This is where wise men became fools and practiced vile affections and deviate sexual shit." Pepe closed his bleary eyes. "Being filled with all unrighteousness," he said, "fornication, wickedness, covetousness, maliciousness; full of envy, murder, debate, deceit, malignity; whisperers, backbiters, haters of God, despiteful, proud, boasters, inventors of evil things."

Pepe opened his eyes, which seemed clearer now. "This is

the spot, *hombre*, believe it. 'Who knowing the judgment of God, that they which commit such things are worthy of death, not only do the same, but have pleasure in them that do them.' God gonna give these sinners *El Gran Beso*, the Big Kiss, pretty quick. You and me, *amigo*, we're lucky, we get to witness.''

"The Big Kiss?"

"Yeah. Kiss can change the world. Could cause a earthquake, firestorm, tidal wave. Who knows? Hey, I can meet her?"

"Meet who?"

"*Su esposa*. Your wife."

"I guess. Right now, though, we're kinda busy. Just stopped over to see about the noises."

"Oh, okay, man."

Pepe Pescuezo squinted at the lowering sun.

"Coolin' down now," he said. "Maybe later we take some *cervezas* together, okay? Tell your wife I meet her soon, man. I go back to sleep, pull the bed away from the wall firs' so I no kick it."

"Hey, thanks."

"*No hay problema*," Pepe said, and closed his door.

Sailor walked back to room six and went inside.

"What's goin' on, Sail?" Lula asked.

"Man waitin' on the Big Kiss, is all."

Lula smiled and threw her arms around Sailor's neck.

"All you boys is alike," she said.

every secret thing

"Any you folks heard about them twenty naked people piled out of a car after it hit a tree in some small town in Louisiana?" Daylight DuRapeau asked the captive passengers as the bus started up 191 toward Tight Fit.

"No? Well, this was a bunch of Pentecostals from Murgatroyd, Texas. Claimed the Lord told 'em to get rid of their worldly belongin's and depart from the Panhandle. Police discovered 'em wanderin' around dazed and nude—men, women, and children. Was on the TV news yesterday. What I'd like to know is how they managed to fit twenty people into one little old car!"

"Dis wiped-out crazy," Baby whispered to Sugargirl. "No way dis happen, no way. Ain' fo' real."

"Hush, chil'," said Sugar. "The Lord find us a way out this mess, we be patient."

Daylight prattled on but Baby tuned her out. She was frightened and missed Jimbo badly. The thought of him coming home from a tough night's work in the refinery and finding her farewell note made her cry. Baby left her tears unwiped.

"You ladies scared?"

Both Baby and Sugargirl looked behind them and saw a

young, good-looking Asian man leaning his head forward over the back of their seat.

"We uneasy," said Sugargirl.

The man smiled. "Me, too," he said. "My name is Crispus Attucks Chew. I'm an engineering student at Georgia Tech. Got on at Atlanta."

"This here's Baby, an' I'm Sugargirl. We comin' from New Orleans. What kinda name is that you got?"

"My father, who's from Shanghai, named me after the first person to die during the American Revolution: Crispus Attucks, a black man. He wanted me to be a real American, since I was born here, in New York City. Everybody calls me Cris."

"Where your daddy at now, Cris?"

"Jersey City, New Jersey. That's where I'm headed. My folks own a restaurant there."

"You know any kind karate?" asked Baby. "Be like Bruce Lee an' get us out dis fix?"

Cris Chew grinned and said, "No, sorry, I don't. I was thinking that when we get to wherever it is she's taking us, we'll have a chance to escape. If we try anything now, plenty of people could get hurt."

"Best we wait, then," said Sugar.

"Hope she don't start shootin'," said Baby.

"Peoples use guns now easy as they used to spit. Other day was a gal go into a twenty-four-hour diner in California two in the A.M., had four of her own children with her, ages six months to six years. No sooner they settled down, the woman, who's only twenty-two years old, lights up a cigarette. Some womens at a table nearby reques' she put it out, bein' they in a no smokin' section. The woman who's smokin' tell 'em mind they own business, but they get the manager who tells her she want to stay, she got to move or stop smokin'.

"Woman got nasty, then, an' begin yellin' insults at the person ask her to stop smokin' in the firs' place. Then she take her kids an' leave the place. She drive home, which is close by, get a gun, go back—the children still with her—an' shoot an' kill one the women, wound another."

"Jesus!" said Crispus Attucks Chew.

"Jesus won't want no part of it," said Sugar. " 'Wisdom is better than weapons,' Ecclesiastes say. 'One sinner destroyeth much good.' "

"Don't take nothin' fo' granted no more," said Baby. "Whole world be up in da air."

Sugargirl leaned back heavily in her seat and closed her eyes.

"For God shall bring every work into judgment," she said, "with every secret thing, whether it be good, or whether it be evil."

"Wow!" Cris said.

"Somethin' for you to chew on," said Sugar.

NO BARGAIN TO BEGIN WITH

"See that?"

"What?" asked Sailor.

"Message painted on the tailgate of that pickup ahead," said Pepe Pescuezo.

Sailor and Lula read the words BELEEVE ON JESUS + BEE SAVE written in bright red letters on the back of an old beige Dodge being driven slowly in front of Sailor's Buick Limited.

"Yeah, so?" said Lula. "Never no shortage of religious persuasion goin' on."

"Bet who's drivin', that *hombre*, he relax in his esoul."

"Not *esoul*," Lula corrected Pepe Pescuezo, "just *soul*. There ain't no letter E in it."

Lula shook a Camel from the pack on the dash, stuck it between her lips, and lit it. She took a couple of drags, then passed it to Sailor.

"So why's this Tight Fit so special?" she asked.

"Is the Holy Spot," said Pepe. "The place on the road to Corinth that Pablo the Apostle stopped at and had his epiphany."

"He was a gagger?" Sailor said.

"What you mean, a gagger?" asked Pepe.

"Had fits where you roll on the ground frothin' at the mouth and could bite off your tongue."

"Sail, honey, no," said Lula. "That's epilepsy. Havin' a epileptic fit from some type trouble with the brain."

"*Epilepsia, si!*" said Pepe.

"An epiphany," Lula continued, "is kinda like a vision, I think. A revelation."

"*Si, si, una revelación!* Tight Fit, it's where Pablo slept the night before he arrive in Corinth, where he had his *sueño grandioso*, the dream of the Most Wicked City. Pablo believe he could save the peoples of Corinth through his ministry."

"Did he?" asked Sailor.

Pepe Pescuezo laughed. "No way, man. This place was worse even than Bagdad."

"You mean in Arabia?" said Lula.

"Naw, in Mexico, near Matamoros. Also was call Boca del Rio. It's where all the smugglers were durin' the time of your Civil War. Tejános, Mexicanos, French, Germans, British was all there, dealin' in *el mercado negro*. Was the *puerto* from where the southern cotton was eship to Europe. An' the *padrones* was fightin' aroun' there, too—*las Banderas Amarillas y las Banderas Rojas*—also los Apaches and Kickapoos, who was terrorizin' along the border. The whole city was fill by gamblers, army deserters, *espies, putas.*"

"Never heard of no Bagdad, Mexico," said Sailor.

"It ain't there no more. Soon after the Civil War end, a *huracán* come an' blow it all away."

"A hurricane?" said Lula.

"*Si. La ciudad del Diablo*, was call. *El Infierno.*"

Sailor zipped the Buick around the Dodge pickup. An old couple, a man and a woman, were riding in it, both wearing wide-brimmed straw hats and blue-lensed sunglasses. Neither of them turned to look at the Buick as Sailor, Lula, and Pepe sped by. When Sailor saw a sign that said Tight Fit Pop. 280, he slowed the car down.

"Know where we're goin', exactly, Pepe?"

"Suppose to be on a hill lookin' over the town. Maybe bes' we estop at a *bodega* and ask."

Sailor drove on a bit farther, until Lula shouted, "Look up there!"

Sailor pulled the Buick over on the road shoulder and applied the brake. Lula pointed to a gray-black cliffside and read aloud the words that had been painted on it in huge white block letters:

" 'IS ANY AMONG YOU AFFLICTED? LET HIM PRAY.— JAMES 5:13.' "

Pepe Pescuezo crossed himself with his right hand, kissed his fingertips, and said, "*Madre de Dios*, this is what my poor brother, Zopo, say always. Mus' be we close to the Holy Spot."

"What's the matter with him?" asked Lula.

"*Mi hermano* was born *jorobado*, a hunchback. His real name was Martín, but everyone call him Zopo, deformed. He was murdered in his bed by two *drogadictos* who broke into our mother's house to steal things. They tortured Zopo, mi *pobrecito*. Stabbed him in his hump with their daggers. Zopo was only eighteen years old, a gentle boy."

"Shit, Pepe, that's terrible!" said Sailor. "Well, guess we ought just head on into the town center, if there is one." He steered the Buick back onto the highway.

"Sure didn't bargain on there bein' so much ugliness in life," Lula said.

"Grandpap Ripley used always to say life weren't no bargain to begin with," said Sailor. "Guess there's no good reason the end ought to be any different."

"Least we can say a prayer for Zopo, we get to the Holy Spot," said Lula.

"*Gracias*," said Pepe. "I know his esoul be save."

SATAN'S SPACESHIP

"Strange, you know," said Cris Chew, "I read about a kidnapping just before I got on this bus."

"Dis ain' no bus," said Baby, "dis be Satan's spaceship."

"Kidnappin' prob'ly the oldes' crime they is," Sugargirl said. "We all be prisoners of some kind, anyhow."

"This was an Aborigine mummy that was found in a funeral home in Cleveland. Apparently, the Aborigine was kidnapped in Australia over a century before by a freak-show agent for the Barnum & Bailey Circus and taken to America."

"Shit," said Baby, "same as slaves."

"Yeah," Cris said. "The Aborigine was named Tambo Tambo and made to throw boomerangs. The freak trader listed his profession as an Australian Cannibal Manager."

"How'd it get in Cleveland?" Baby asked.

"Guess Tambo Tambo died there in a hotel, when the circus was passing through, and just got left behind. The article said the corpse had been embalmed twice. It was found in the basement of a mortuary that was about to be torn down."

"What gone happen to it?"

"The Australian government said they were prepared to

bring Tambo Tambo back once his descendants decide what to do with the remains."

"Lord knows what gone remain of us," said Baby, "dis crazy woman finish."

The bus slowed and turned down a winding road off the highway. Daylight directed the driver along a circuitous, tree-lined stretch until they arrived at a dead-end clearing, where-upon she instructed him to stop.

"This be the spot," she announced to the passengers. " 'Behold, a whirlwind of the Lord is gone forth in fury . . . it shall fall grievously upon the head of the wicked.' Open the door, driver. Ever'body out now, an' y'all watch yo' step."

In the middle of the clearing stood a tiny Asian woman wearing a black motorcycle jacket and dark glasses. Seated in a semicircle around her were eighteen women ranging in age from fifteen to fifty-five. All of the women seated on the ground were dressed in diaphanous yellow costumes that fea-tured wings and antennae.

"What the hell!?" exclaimed Baby Cat-Face, when she saw them.

"Chil'," Sugargirl Crooks said, "don't take this for gospel, but I think we done landed on the planet of the bugs."

LA PUNAISE

Daylight DuRapeau herded the bus passengers, including the driver, together and ordered them to be seated on the ground in the clearing in front of the small Asian woman.

"Welcome," said the woman, without removing her dark glasses. "My name is Imelda Go, and I am the artistic director and cofounder of the H. D. Stanton Institute. These girls and women before you are residents of the institute, which is dedicated to the belief that true art can be created only by those persons society considers radically challenged by so-called consensus reality. We at the institute decided to choose at random a group of outsiders—yourselves, as it has turned out—to witness a performance of our new ballet, La Punaise. That is, of course, the French title, the language in which the master composer, François Noyade, conceived it. In English, it is The Bug. The choreography, c'est moi."

"Oh my, my, my," Sugargirl said to nobody in particular. "What be happenin' here?"

"No talkin'!" commanded Daylight DuRapeau. "Y'all give Miz Go her respec'!"

Two of the costumed women picked up cornets, put these to their lips, and played a few notes.

"Ah!" exclaimed Imelda Go. "The bugles of the bugs!"

The players rose and assembled themselves, wings akimbo, in appropriate positions behind her. As Ms. Go narrated, the women danced.

"Two teenagers, a girl and a boy, are on their way home from school. They are playing hide-and-seek along a path by a river. The girl, Lita, shouts to the boy, 'You're it!' She runs ahead and steps behind a tree as Philip, the boy, runs by. She waits and then sits down, her back against a rock next to an enormous, old, half-dead tree.

"Lita takes off her backpack and pulls out a large red textbook, *The Secret Life of Insects*. The title is written in large gold letters on the cover. She begins to read from the book while nibbling on a sandwich that she has pulled from her pack. Soon she notices a trail of small insects carrying the crumbs from her repast toward an opening in the old tree. Fascinated, she crouches down to take a closer look. Lying down, propped on one elbow, the young girl becomes totally engrossed in the industrious insects. Reality fades into a blur and the tree begins to grow. Or is she shrinking? Lita reclines into a deep sleep.

"She awakens, finding herself in a labyrinth deep inside the earth. As her eyes become accustomed to the strange new light, she finds that she is among many forms of insect life. Lita is at once frightened and amazed by what she sees. Iridescent beetles, delicate ants, and spotted ladybugs twirl and flutter, their transparent wings trailing. They perform dances of play, flirtation, and love. The bugs do not seem to notice Lita observing them, so absorbed are they in their own activities. Two ants draw her attention as their courting dance becomes more sensual. The two creatures bump and writhe, rubbing their armored bodies together. They reach an erotic climax as the walls burst apart. Termite warriors enter the chamber in full battle gear. A melee ensues. The energy level changes from erotic to martial but remains strangely sensual. The insects clash in individual combat. Lita takes cover behind debris from the caved-in wall.

"At the height of the battle, a magnificent Bug Prince—the teenage boy, Philip—rides into the fray atop a stunning green beetle. Brandishing a glowing scepter, he routs the head termite, whose troops follow him in retreat back through the openings in the chamber walls.

"The victorious insects rejoice. Lita, overwhelmed by what she has witnessed, bolts upright from behind the debris and faints at the same moment she is spotted by the Bug Prince. He dismounts the green beetle, sweeps her up with his appendages, and remounts. He carefully observes her; then, to the amazement of all the insects, he rides with her out of the chamber.

"Lita regains consciousness in the Bug Prince's private throne room. She is lying on a couch of fresh mulberry leaves. The Bug Prince is seated on his throne in deep thought, one hand holding a jewel-encrusted goblet. To his right is a lectern upon which lies a large red book. The gold letters on the cover read: *The Secret Life of Insects.*

"Lita gasps and jumps up to flee. The Bug Prince snaps out of his reverie and quickly crosses the room to her side. Lita raises her hands in fright. The Bug Prince, through pantomime, pleads with her to stay, promising she will not be harmed. Lita is touched by his gestures and she decides that he is sincere. She is now drawn to him, and they dance together.

"He tells Lita of his lifelong desire to become human and dwell in The Land Above the Bugs. Lita explains that this is not a good idea, because in the Land Above the Bugs he will no longer be a prince. Lita comforts him, and they assume the grace of impossible lovers, knowing and acknowledging that in their present states they cannot really be together.

"Lita stays with the Bug Prince, however, and begins to read from the big red book, *The Secret Life of Insects.* She turns the large pages, searching for an answer to their dilemma. Suddenly, she comes upon a passage in the book that she believes offers a solution. The book contains a spell that once cast cannot be reversed. It provides for one irrevocable passage to the Land Above the Bugs. Lita reads aloud the spell, and with the use of the magic scepter, brings forth a dense mist that enshrouds both her and the Bug Prince.

"The mist clears and reveals Lita asleep under the old tree, her head resting on her schoolbook. Philip finds her and wakes her up. He is excited and shows her the magic scepter, which he has found by the river. Lita rises and embraces Philip. She touches the scepter and together they dance."

Just as the bug ballet concluded, Sailor, Lula, and Pepe Pescuezo pulled up in the Buick.

"Look!" Cris Chew said to Baby and Sugar, pointing at the car. "Let's run for it!"

The three of them piled into Sailor's Limited and Cris shouted, "Drive, man! Get us outta here!"

Without questioning Cris's command, Sailor wrenched his vehicle into reverse, spun it around, and sped away.

"They ain' followin' us," said Baby Cat-Face, looking out the rear window.

"What's goin' on back there?" asked Lula.

"Girl, you wouldn't believe it if we told you," Sugargirl said. "Best you please jus' give us a spell, recover, you don't mind."

"My daddy went gator huntin' once," Sailor said, as he guided the car back toward the main highway, "down around Immokalee, in the Everglades. Told me he and a fella name of Destrozo Chusma, man he done some county time with he was younger, was out in a airboat with a harpoon gun. Daddy said this Destrozo Chusma, who was half Seminole, harpooned a bull gator direct in the ass, instead of in the head like you're supposed to. Destrozo reeled in the gator and damned if it didn't bite him on the hand. Daddy wanted to get him to a hospital but Destrozo was a tough old boy. Just took a fifth of Cuervo Gold he had in the boat and poured about half of it over the wound, then wrapped his hand with duct tape. Told Daddy he'd have it taken care of proper later. You folks look pretty shook. Take all the time you need."

TOO WICKED FOR WORDS

Lula was awakened by a bloodcurdling scream.

"Sail! Sail!" she said, sitting up in bed. "Did you hear that?"

"Couldn't help it, peanut," Sailor answered, propping himself up on his left elbow and blinking his eyes open. "Sounded like that British guy in Arabia in that movie we seen, when he got took captive and had a hot tire tool shoved up his ass."

"Jesus, Sailor, you would think somethin' uncouth. This noise was too wicked for words."

Sailor and Lula were in their room at the South China Sea Motel. They had stayed up late the night before with Pepe, listening to Baby, Sugar, and Cris relate the story and their impressions of their bizarre ordeal. Sailor got out of bed and began to put on his clothes.

"Sail, where you goin'?"

"See who got their throat cut, prob'ly."

Sailor opened the front door and was immediately confronted by Pepe Pescuezo.

"You hear it, too, huh?"

"Yeah, Pepe. You know which room it come from?"

"I think *Señorita Bebé Gata y Señora Azúcar.*"

Sailor and Pepe went to room seven and knocked on the door.

Sugargirl Crooks opened it and said, "Yes, Lord, it was her. 'Lift up thy feet unto the perpetual desolations; even all that the enemy hath done wickedly in the sanctuary. Thine enemies roar in the midst of thy congregations.' "

Baby Cat-Face was still in bed, her head and back resting on pillows.

"I was jus' tryin' to get yesterday out of my mouth," she said.

THE SHADOW OF EGYPT

"Jimbo, sweetie, it's me."

"Baby! Where you at?"

"Carolina, honey. Motel call the South China Sea."

"I been missin' you so bad, Baby. When you comin'
home?"

"Takin' the Southern Trail at midnight. Call my aunt Graciela an' turn out she up in Chicago visitin' Cousin Roscoe,
her son now call himself Majeed. Shoulda check before I
come, I guess, but I was crazy to jus' get."

"I know, Baby."

"Lord, Jimbo, you wouldn't believe what all been happen.
Firs', bus get hijack by a bigass sister wid a machine rifle."

"Esquerita, you okay? Baby, tell me you okay."

"I'm okay, Jimbo, but jus' listen what else. I hook up wid
guess who?"

"Who?"

"Sugargirl Crooks!"

"You serious? Gal sung 'Dude Don't Get Much Res' When
He Be Sleepin' Aroun'?' "

"She on the bus wid us. But dig, darlin', dis big mama
make the driver detour to a place where a Oriental lady

midget name Imelda Go got a buncha half-mental girls in bug costumes be makin' a ballet!"

"Shit, Baby! Say what?"

"Dis ain' no bull, Jimbo. We was kidnap so dey have 'em a audience."

"Don' make no sense."

"Don' need tell me dat! But it happen. Finally, we was rescue'. Sugar, Chinaboy from New York name Cris Chew, an' me."

"Who by?"

"Some young white folks, boy an' girl name Sailor an' Lula, an' a Mexican name Pepe. Happen they come along lookin' for da Holy Spot."

"Baby, maybe bes' I get da details you get back home. I already confuse'."

"Easy be confuse' these days, Mister Deal."

"Peoples be puttin' they faith in false prophets, Baby, 'stead of the Lord. Why they lost and uncertain. As Isaiah say, 'Therefore shall the strength of Pharaoh be your shame, an' the trust in the shadow of Egyp' your confusion.' "

"I trust you, Jimbo. Ashame' I lef'."

"Baby Cat-Face, I be there to meet the bus."

Live Bodies

Baby Cat-Face descended the steps from the Southern Trails bus and fell into the big arms of Jimbo Deal.

"Oh, Jimbo," she said, snail trails staining her mahogany cheeks, "I decide on the way, I ain' never gon' quit you again."

"You know how glad I am to hear you say dat, darlin'."

After they were back in their apartment on Martinique Alley, Jimbo Deal sat next to Baby Cat-Face on the fake-leopard-skin sofa.

"Esquerita, I do got somethin' less'n fine to tell ya."

"Oh, Jimbo, what?"

"Tricky gone."

"Tricky gone? What you mean?"

"I mean, she dead. She been kill. Police found her body day before yesterday. Smother to death, they say."

"Aw, no. Jimbo, what really happen?"

"Got the article from the paper."

Jimbo took a clipping from the breast pocket of his brown guayabera shirt and read aloud.

" 'A woman identify as Miguelita "Tricky" Divine was foun' Saturday in da John Sinclair Public Housin' Complex. An autopsy show she had been smother to death. The woman had been dead three to seven days when she was foun' partially nude in a stairwell about two-thirty P.M., chief coroner's spokesman Deuce Coupée said. The thirty-five-year-old woman's body was identify by two tattoos: "TRICKY" on her inner right forearm, an' "SWEET LIL ANGEL" on her inner right thigh.' "

"That Tricky, sure."

" 'She also had a vertical—' "

"What that?"

"Vertical mean up an' down, 'stead of runnin' across. 'She also had a vertical surgical scar on her stomach, an' a gold cap upper right tooth wid a cutout of a star.' "

"Tricky widout no doubt."

" 'Her neighbors at da housin' complex could provide no information on who might have commit da murder, which is da sixty-third reported homicide in da city dis year.' "

"Shit, Jimbo, I can't stand dis no more. New Orleans jus' too violen' for me."

"Don' soun' like things any better in North Carolina. Where you propose to go?"

Baby curled up in Jimbo's lap, allowing him to cradle her against his chest.

"Don' know. Suppose they ain' really no place folks like us can go. Prob'ly bes' I jus' put my trus' in you, Mister Deal."

"An mine in you, Miz Bug. 'Bout all a live body can do."

"Oh, darlin', I love when you call me bug, even though I seen a strange sight involvin' bugs in Carolina."

Outside the window two gunshots went off, followed by the sound of people running. Baby Cat-Face held on hard to Jimbo Deal.

PURiFieD

Dear Sugargirl.

I owe you a letter let you now what I doin back in NO. Jimbo bein bes to me he ever hav. I tol him all what happin an how you an me an the China from New York wood probly be dead didn Sailorboy an Lula an Pep come by. I now defitly I needen somp mor in my life an now I found it. I join Mother Bizco Temple of the Few Wash Pure By Her Blood. Revern Mother Fenomena Bizco our pastor she take in junky hos an young girls need abortin get em medical care then puts em to work. I workin for her fi days a week somtime six or sevn. Coleck funs an perform all sorts charty works. She bout the bes preacher you ever here. Talk about her mama Virguenza Bizco y Fea give birth her dauter by hersef without nobody attenden duren blue moon of Septembr wen shes 17. Virguenza be blin sins age of 7 follow fall from a diseas chinabery tree. She was rape in St Louis cemetary number 2 by 4 skimask yahoos from Alabama be in NO for Sugar bowl say yella pusy rednek idea lagnap. Virguenza ain never tol her parents wat happin bein chuby begin wit the baby don show an she return to St Louis cemetary number 2 hav the child. Wen she turn up home wit it say she find her baby abandon cryin in a trash can.

Virguenza mama Katy Jurado Bizco they part spanish cordn to Mother Bizco xclam que fenomena wich is how her girl come to be name Fenomena. Inclos a card nex time you in NO I take you fo sure. Mother Bizco do such good work Sug you be mihty impres she got more storys den enny 1. Even Jimbo come on Sundy. Mos now I work wit Aid peepls prefur die at home in they on bed I don blam em. Lord have mercy on em an us Sug Mother Bizco say nobody xcap.

Love

Baby

```
        MOTHER BIZCO'S TEMPLE OF THE
     FEW WASHED PURE BY HER BLOOD
        2308 1/2 Burgundy Street
          New Orleans 17, La.

  REVEREND MOTHER FENÓMENA BIZCO, Pastor

    "And when the ship was caught,
   and could not bear up into the wind,
         we let HER drive."
          --THE ACTS, 27:15
```

INTERLUDE:
THE ASSASSIN'S LAST LETTER

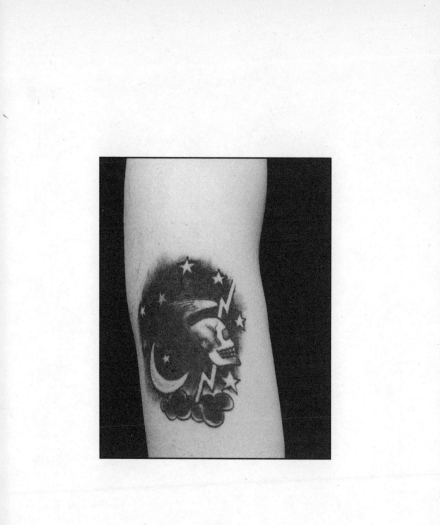

Dear Son,
I have been singing this song lately.

> Oh Mammy, Mammy tell me,
> Why do they call me Snowball?
> Why do they call me Snowball
> when Snowball ain't my name?
> My mommy calls me Sugarplum,
> my daddy calls me Appledump.
> Oh Mammy, Mammy ain't it a shame
> when Snowball ain't my name.

When I was a boy my mama would sing it to me most nights. She was drunken she couldn't, then I'd sing it to myself. Never have forgot the words. Funny tune, isn't it? Always I could picture that pickaninny rocking on his mammy's knee, asking. Way it is in life, though, some folks knowing and others always and forever wondering why. You know I am an educated man, high school plus two years of college. I have read so many books but the only book where the answers are available, the answers to every question, is the Old Testament, the one and only truly Good Book.

As Moses wrote in Numbers, when men of the Lost Tribe began to consort with nigger whores and bow down to false gods, the Lord said unto Moses, Take all the heads of the people and hang them up before Me against the sun. And Moses said unto the judges of Israel, Slay ye every one his men that were joined unto Baalpeor. Then Zimri, one of the tribe, brought home a darkie bitch named Cozbi, front of Moses and everyone, right in their face. When Phinehas, the son of Eleazar and grandson of Aaron, saw this, he took up his javelin, followed Zimri and his Midianite whore into their tent, and thrust both of them through, the woman in her belly. Because Phinehas so acted, the plague that killed twenty and four thousand was stayed from the children of Israel. The Lord rewarded Phinehas with the covenant of an everlasting priesthood.

Phinehas is the inspiration for right-thinking Caucasian men, the vanguard assassin of the enemies of God. He knew his duty without being told what to do. This helped make it possible for the Lost Tribe to find their way out of the wilderness, to depart from Moab and head north through the Caucasus Mountains to Scandinavia and the British Isles. The Israelites were Caucasians, those who crossed the mountains, and their descendants, the Anglo-Saxons, are the true Chosen People. You are one. The Jews are numbered only in satan's synagogue, along with the niggers. As Phinehas heeded the Lord's disapproval of miscegenation and slew Zimri and Cozbi, so is it meant that His Chosen Sons behave.

I am telling you this so you understand I am no mean individual, that any acts of violence I committed were as that of Phinehas and sanctioned by the will of God. When the

Lord told Moses to decapitate those sinners and string their heads up against the sun, He meant men to know His word was law. When Phinehas smote the whoremonger and his darkie, like they claim I murdered Miguelita Tricky Divine, the Lord *blessed* him. I am *informed* by God, dispatched by Him to do battle with the mud races and rid the earth of satan's offspring.

They can execute me but they cannot defeat my Soul, for I am as Jeremiah: the Lord is with me as a mighty terrible one, therefore my persecutors shall stumble, and they shall not prevail. They shall be greatly ashamed, for they shall not prosper and their everlasting confusion shall never be forgotten.

See you in Heaven, Son

Dad

MOTHER BiZCO'S TEMPLE OF THE FEW WASHED PURE BY HER BLOOD

BUZZARD'S LUCK

Sister Esquerita took the .30/06 caliber 1917 Enfield rifle fitted with a six-power Golden Hawk telescopic sight and held it up for everyone to see. As usual for Sunday night's sermon, more than five hundred people were in the temple to witness Mother Bizco's testimony.

"The very weapon, people, employed by the murderer Ezra Nuez when he struck down in the coldest blood our own Brother Sheshbazar. Thank you, Sister Esquerita. You may now return the instrument of destruction to safekeeping."

Sister Esquerita departed the stage as Mother Bizco continued.

"As most of you already know, we at the Temple of the Few Washed Pure by Her Blood have cleansed the world of this assassin Nuez. We take care of our own business, needing no service of outsiders."

"Amen!" chorused the congregation.

"Now there was a certain man of Elohim, of Mount Toil, and his name was Desire, the son of Love, the son of Vainglory, the son of Right-Thinking, the son of Over-and-Back, an In-Time man."

"Hallelujah!"

"And he had two wives. The name of the one was Honor, and the name of the other Pain. And Pain had children, but Honor had no children."

"Hallelujah!"

"And this man went up out of his city yearly to worship and to sacrifice unto the Lord of hosts in Denial. And the two sons of Offal, Fill-It and Do-Wrong, the priests of the Lord, were there."

"Hallelujah!"

"And when the time was that Desire offered, he gave to Pain, his wife, and to all her sons and her daughters, permission to take revenge when necessary."

"Hallelujah!"

"But unto Honor he spoke of forgiveness in all things. This way did Desire cover his ample posterior."

"Hallelujah!"

As Mother Bizco sermonized, Sister Esquerita, known to intimates by her nickname, Baby Cat-Face, locked away the rifle in the temple's weapons chest and stole out the side door of the building into Spain Street to light up a cigarette. She leaned back against the brown bricks and inhaled deeply. As she exhaled, tears flowed from her eyes. Late that afternoon, Baby had learned she was pregnant for sure, a situation that would not mix, considering the vow of chastity she had taken when she became a full-time sister to Mother Bizco. As a member of the temple's Almost-Perfect Flock, Sister Esquerita was expected to devote her entire being to the furtherance of charity as defined by Mother Bizco's book; to give herself up to pure works. Baby had instead given herself up, in what Mother Bizco would define as an unreasoning moment of unheavenly forgetfulness, to a funky piece of the devil's work called Waldo Orchid, an acquaintance of her former boyfriend Jimbo Deal.

"Jus' my luck," Baby Cat-Face confided to the wet air.

Esquerita's tears mingled with sweat hoovered from her pores by the unholy heat that crept up in the summer from the Amazon Basin to New Orleans.

"Buzzard's luck," she said, then took a long drag on her Kool and closed her eyes, letting the bitter water drip down her face and into her mouth as she moaned.

" 'My soul is continually in my hand, yet I do not forget the law. The wicked have laid a snare for me.' "

A giant cockroach scooted up the wall next to Baby and she scrunched it with the fiery end of the Kool.

WALDO REGRETS

Waldo Orchid lived in a shotgun bungalow on Lapeyrouse Street with his widowed mother, Malva, and his spinster Tante Desuso, Malva's older sister. Waldo's father, Tosco Orchid, had died when Waldo, his only child, was six. Tosco, an electrician, had been rewiring the tower of the Lighthouse for the Blind building on Camp Street when a sepia-puce Norway rat the size of an average javelina exploded from a dark corner of the crawl space Tosco had wedged himself into and sank its diseased incisors into Tosco's carotid artery. The elder Orchid had bled to death even before he could extricate himself from the cubbyhole.

This paternal loss so enervated the juvenile Orchid that until the age of fifteen he barely ate. Waldo was such a skinny kid, and had such a prominent overbite, that, to his horror, he became known in the neighborhood as Rat Boy. In an effort to eradicate this image of himself, Waldo began to eat upon waking and continued until bedtime every day. By the age of twenty, the former Rat Boy stood five foot nine and weighed 325 pounds; even then, upon self-appraisal in a mirror, Waldo thought he could do with some fattening up.

It was a steamy gray morning when Baby knocked on the

door of the house on Lapeyrouse Street. Tante Desuso, whom Baby had never met, opened up a crack and said, "What you wan'?"

Baby was startled by the old woman's eyes, which in the dimness appeared to be perfectly yellow.

"Is Waldo Orchid at home?"

"He is, he sleep. Who wanna know?"

"My name is Esquerita Reyna. *Sister* Esquerita."

"Sister? From what church?"

"Temple da Few Wash Pure by Her Blood, down Burgundy in da Marigny."

"Dat crackpot quadroon Mother Bizco's church, ain' it?"

"Yes, ma'am. But Mother Bizco ain' no crackpot. She help all sorts of folks."

"Our Lady da Holy Fantômes where we belong."

"Yes, ma'am. Can you see Waldo be in? Tell him Baby need to see him."

"*Baby?* Who dat?"

"Be me."

"Thought you was Sister Esquerita Raymon'."

"Reyna, mean queen. I am, but he know me by my familiar name."

Tante Desuso closed the door. Baby waited on the porch and thought about the night she had backslid and gotten nasty on Crown Royal with Waldo and his one-legged Hungarian-Creole partner, Balzac Kicz. Baby had encountered the two men in Elgrably's Grocery on Mandeville, around the corner from the temple, where she had gone to buy cigarettes. Waldo Orchid had introduced himself, reminding her that they had met once before at the Evening in Seville Bar on Lesseps Street, back when she cribbed with Jimbo Deal. Orchid and Deal had both belonged to the Lost Tribe of Venus Pleasure & Social Club on Claiborne before it burned down under mysterious circumstances two Christmases back. Baby remembered Jimbo saying that a former member named Bambola Schmid, who had been thrown out for welshing on card debts, was suspected of having torched the building. Bambola had disappeared from New Orleans after the fire and apparently found a haven with cousins who operated a hotel in the Swiss Alps named Die Müssigkeit. Nobody from the Lost Tribe had been able to get to Switzerland to verify this, however.

Waldo then introduced Baby to his pal Balzac Kicz, and they invited her to join them for a beverage. The two men were extremely polite, and since Baby had no duties that afternoon, and no plans in particular, she went along with the strange pair to Enrique's Birdcage on Almonaster Avenue.

What happened after that Baby had mostly dismissed from her cerebrum. Blasted as she had been on Crown Royal, she now remembered only her mirthful reaction to Waldo Orchid's obesity necessitating that she mount him in order to sufficiently effect intercourse. Baby had not had sexual relations of any kind since she and Jimbo had split up, and Waldo caught her at a weak moment. She was certain, however, that she had not been intimate with the rail-thin and gimpy Balzac Kicz. As far as she could recall, Kicz had injected himself hypodermically in his remaining ankle with a purplish substance he referred to as "cobra come." The Magyar druggie then passed out in the bathroom of his apartment on General Diaz, to which the trio had repaired following the frivolities at Enrique's Birdcage.

Baby had dated Waldo Orchid twice since that night, and on one occasion he showed her where he lived, although they had not gone inside the house. Waldo told Baby that he and Balzac Kicz were weapons importers, most of their product coming from China, and the majority of their sales being made to the white religious right in Idaho and black separatists in California. After her last secret date with Waldo a month or so before, Baby had decided to end their association, such as it was, mainly because of her guilt about transgressing Mother Bizco's dictum that her Almost-Perfect Flock abstain from alcohol, drugs, and sex. The other reason was that Waldo had backhanded her across the mouth after she refused to give him beso negro. All she wanted of him now was money for an abortion.

The door cracked open and Tante Desuso said, "Waldo regrets he unable to talk today." Then she closed it again.

Baby Cat-Face stepped down from the porch and into Lapeyrouse Street. A few raindrops hit her, a breeze came up, and then a platinum bolt of ribbon lightning discharged about twenty-five coulombs of negative energy from the N-region of a cumulus cloud into the ground directly in front of her, the force of which knocked Esquerita flat but not out. Next came an almost deafening bang, followed by a torrent of water that totally soaked the prone *enceinte*.

Baby lay on the sidewalk with her eyes closed, allowing the rain to cleanse her body. She shouted out, "Deliver me, O Lord, from the evil man! Preserve me from the violent man who have purposed to overthrow my goings!"

There came another thunderclap, and Baby whispered, "I call heaven and earth to witness against you this day, Waldo Orchid, that ye shall soon perish from off the land. Ye shall not prolong your days upon it, but shall utterly be destroyed."

ReVeLATIoNS

Baby Cat-Face considered going to Mother Bizco with her problem, but decided that the revelation would preclude the Sister's ever again being deemed worthy of what Mother called "a balance beyond trust," and most certainly would result in expulsion from the temple's Almost-Perfect Flock.

"That's what I be, though," Baby said aloud to herself, "*almos' poifec'*."

Sister Esquerita lay on the narrow bed in her room in the attic of the temple, listening to rain gust against the window. A big storm was blowing in. An early-season hurricane had already hit hard around Pinar del Río, Cuba, turned north-northwest, and was presently pushing steadily toward the Mississippi Gulf Coast and Louisiana.

Baby fell asleep and dreamed that she was wandering alone through a big city, someplace she had never been. The streets were entirely deserted, though everything seemed in working order: stoplights and clocks functioned, but there were no birds, no pedestrians, no traffic. She seemed to be the only living thing on earth. A red hatbox appeared in front of her on the sidewalk. Baby stopped and opened it and saw her own head, eyes closed, lying on a bed of golden lettuce. The eyes opened and in a deep voice that was not hers, Baby's head said, "This shall be a sign unto you, that the pride of thine heart hath deceived thee. But now, my daughter, fear not. I will do to thee all that thou requirest, for all of the city of my people doth know that thou art a virtuous woman. Take the shield of faith wherewith ye shall be able to quench all the fiery darts of the wicked. Your child shall be my child, and his sword shall be my sword, and the slain shall be many. He shall go forth like a whirlwind to render his anger with fury. Your enemies shall be as mine own, and it shall come to pass that his acts shall be as my acts. He will be a wild man, his hand will be against every man, and every man's hand against him."

Baby was awakened by a crash of thunder. She stared at the spiderleg cracks in the ceiling and held tight with both hands to the sides of her bed, which began to rock from side to side. Esquerita felt as if she were being torn from the bed by an unseen force, and then her body was above it, levitating, her fingers grasping desperately for purchase. She was on her back in midair, halfway between ceiling and bed, frightened in a way she never could have imagined possible. Baby heard the water, the wind, and then she heard a voice similar to the one that had spoken in her dream.

"Hear me, mother, for I am your son, and my name is Angel de la Cruz. My life shall be your protection and glory. The fearful and unbelieving, the abominable, the murderers and whoremongers, the sorcerers and idolators, and all liars, shall drown in the lake which burneth with fire and sulfur. Wipe away all tears from your eyes, for there shall be no more pain upon you. The former things are passed away."

Sister Esquerita slept again, and when she awoke she lay on her bed, bathed in a finger of rosy light. She placed both of her hands on her belly, caressed herself, and whispered his name, "Angel, Angel de la Cruz."

iN THE LiNE OF FiRE

Fenómena Bizco was born in Quincy, Florida, the fourth daughter of Vasco da Gama Bizco y Caprichoso and Cora Roosevelt. Her parents worked as migrant fruit and vegetable pickers and were, at the time of Fenómena's birth, gathering strawberries. Vasco da Gama had come to the United States from Arco Iris, Cuba, and met his future wife in a peach orchard outside of Tampa. Bizco was twenty-two years old and already considered himself a minister in what he called La Iglesia del Espíritu Santo Viajero, or the Church of the Holy Ghost Traveler. He converted the fourteen-year-old Cora Roosevelt, who had been raised an African Disciple of Paul, married her, and together they preached the gospel according to Vasco da Gama Bizco in migrant camps across the Deep South.

Bizco's belief was that the Holy Ghost protected poor people and guarded their souls against theft by the rich, thereby ensuring their only true means of salvation. Each of Vasco and Cora's first three daughters died almost immediately after birth. That their fourth survived Vasco considered a genuine phenomenon, and named her appropriately. Fenómena had no formal education, learning only what her parents taught her, which was mainly Vasco's interpretation of the Old Testament as it related to current events.

When Fenómena was sixteen, both Vasco and Cora were crushed to death by a crop-dusting plane as they slept in their tent in a pickers' camp close by a cotton field in Lillian, Alabama. Fenómena escaped death only because she had sneaked away after her parents had fallen asleep in order to tryst with a beautiful deaf boy named Sordo Perobello. When the plane's engine conked out, causing the Cessna to suddenly dive and crumple on the Bizcos and many others, Sordo did not stop pumping away at Fenómena, who was pinned firmly beneath him. Despite her attempts to push him off, Sordo's superior strength and fierce concentration on the matter at hand kept her from immediately aiding her parents. Not until fuel leaked from the downed duster's fuselage and sparked an explosion did Sordo desist, it being impossible to ignore the white ball of flame that instantly transformed night into day.

Following this tragedy, Fenómena continued toiling as a migrant picker for several months until a girl named Viridiana Temoign told her she knew of a way they could make a lot more money without working so hard. Viridiana, a fifteen-year-old runaway from Daytime, Arkansas, convinced Fenómena that fucking for cash and clothes in New Orleans would be a better deal than plucking fruit and getting their asses scraped and soiled while giving it away for free to half-wits in cotton fields, and together they split for the City That Care Forgot.

So began Vasco da Gama and Cora Bizco's only surviving progeny's sojourn as a prostitute, a path that led her into heroin addiction and a life of fear. Never during her many years of enslavement to Satan, Fenómena told those who came under the sound of her voice at the Temple of the Few Washed Pure by Her Blood, did a day pass when she was not afraid. Only after her return to the teachings she had first heard from her father in the peripatetic Church of the Holy Ghost Traveler did Fenómena force Satan to relinquish his horny-handed hold on her soul. She had snatched it back from him in the hour before dawn of a new and glorious day as she lay in a puddle of her own filth in a cell at the Orleans Parish jail. It was desperation that put her there in the first place, Fenómena preached, and desperation that took her out.

"Raise up!" Mother Bizco called to her flock and those not yet converted. "Raise up out of the slime and degradation the devil desire to drown you in! Gettin' down ain't no unforgivable sin! Despair the onliest unforgivable sin, and it always reachin' for us! Get out that trick bag and take hold of your soul! The Holy Ghost wash you clean, an' be with you wherever you go!"

When Sister Esquerita confronted Mother Bizco with the truth of her situation, and related the experience of her epiphany and the coming of her son, Angel de la Cruz, Fenómena embraced the Almost-Perfect acolyte and told her, "Child, the Holy Ghost is come upon you. He descended in a bodily shape like a dove, and a voice came from heaven, which said, 'Thou art my beloved Son; in thee I am well pleased.' "

Later, back in her room, after she had been brought before the congregation by Mother Bizco, received a public blessing, and been pronounced an Immaculate Receptacle, Sister Esquerita could not keep from laughing out loud at the thought of Waldo Orchid as a dove.

"Don't care what Mother Bizco say," Baby promised herself, "one kinda way or another that fat-ass motherfucker gon' pay a *serious* price!"

WHITE NARCISSUS

Baby was bothered throughout her pregnancy by a recurring dream in which she relived each moment of her final sexual encounter with Waldo Orchid. The hotel room he had rented for the purpose was dark, lit only by intermittent flashes of lightning from the thunderstorm that raged outside. As Waldo had instructed her to do, Baby stripped off her clothes in the living room of the suite and walked into the bedroom, where Waldo waited, seated on the bed. Waldo was wearing a turban and was naked to the waist, his flabby lower body wrapped in a gold lamé skirt.

"Ah, the white narcissus," said Waldo, when he saw her.

Baby went to the closet and took out a gold lamé robe with a long train. She half-wrapped the robe about her, then took down a hatbox from a shelf, from which she removed a long-tressed golden wig.

"Go 'head, darlin'," Waldo said, "put it on."

Baby fitted the wig on her head, adjusted the robe, and turned toward Waldo.

"That good?"

"Baby, you poifec'."

"No, only almos'."

Waldo slid off the bed and dropped to his knees in front of Baby Cat-Face. She began to dance and swirl around him, the thunder and lightning accentuating and punctuating her movements and gestures. Baby twirled the train and Waldo let it fall over his head and shoulders. He picked up the end of it and kissed the material tenderly, caressed it with his fingers, and rubbed it around his swollen breasts. As Baby continued her sinuous dance, which Waldo had choreographed in advance, he whimpered and writhed and crawled around her, seemingly in an attempt to inhabit the lamé by burying his head in it.

"Princess! Princess! I am drowning in your ocean! Help me, princess! Save me!"

"There is a flower, a white flower, the white narcissus," said Baby, repeating the words Waldo had made her memorize. "If you can find the flower, the fluted lips of the flower, the princess will sing."

"Oh, my princess, my lovely, lovely flower. Keep me near you, keep me, keep me, swallow me!"

Baby allowed Waldo to twine himself around her legs like a serpent. As he did, together they repeated the litany, "Keep me, swallow me! Keep me, swallow me! Keep me, swallow me!"

Waldo discarded the turban, buried his head beneath Baby's robe, and moved his head up between her legs.

"Say it now, Baby!" Waldo ordered. "Sing to me!"

> "Canst thou not tell me of a gentle pair
> That likest thy Narcissus are?
> O, if thou have
> Hid them in some flowery cave,
> Tell me but where."

As Baby repeated these lines, Waldo made love to her, pulling the little Esquerita onto his lap, where she collapsed over him, riding out her own fever to the thunderous accompaniment of the storm.

When Baby awoke from this dream, she would be drenched in sweat and overwhelmed by a need to vomit, which she would into a pot she kept for this purpose on the floor beside her bed. Baby had never asked Waldo why he wanted her to participate in this peculiar routine. Neither did she ask what the words meant that he made her recite, although Waldo did tell her afterward that they were from a poem by a dead Englishman named Milton. Baby was not surprised to learn that Waldo read poetry; it was just further proof of her belief that he was by far the weirdest person she had ever known.

BAD DUDES

Balzac Kicz corkscrewed his way through the Saturday night crowd in Ruby's Caribbean Bar until he reached the door in the rear marked DU ES. He pushed it open, entered, and limped up to a vacant urinal. Standing next to him was a heavyset black man who had his eyes closed as he pissed. The two were alone in the restroom.

"Keep paying 'em, don't we?" Balzac asked.

"Say wha'?" said the man.

"What it says on the door to here: D-U-E-S. The second D is dropped off, so instead of dudes, says dues. Even doing so simple a thing as to take a pee, we are reminded."

"Mm, mm," the man mumbled, his eyes still closed as he rocked back on his heels, then tilted forward so far that his forehead bumped against the wall where a cretin had carved the words JESUS DESERVED IT.

"Hey, fella, you all right?" asked Kicz.

"Mm, mm," he said.

The man then collapsed to the floor. Balzac interrupted his own micturition and knelt next to him. Kicz saw that the man, who appeared to be unconscious, was still holding his empurpled penis in his right hand. Balzac bent down and began to fellate his fallen piss-mate. Just as Balzac Kicz's own organ elongated, the door opened.

"Hey!" yelled the tall, skinny white man who had entered. "What you doin' on Jimbo?"

Before Balzac could stand, the tall, skinny man, who wore a T-shirt proclaiming JIMI IS LORD, and whose exposed arms were littered with crude tattoos, mostly of women in various degrees of nudity, grabbed the Hungarian-Creole junkie-pervert by the neck and pulled him up.

"Listen, I . . . ," Kicz stuttered.

"Fuckin' faggot!" shouted the man, who then proceeded to pummel him.

As Balzac attempted to escape, his wooden left leg disengaged and clattered to the floor next to where Jimbo, oblivious to the situation, snoozed in benign repose. Jimbo's self-appointed savior picked up the loose limb, held it in both hands, and beat Balzac with it until the plastic cracked and splintered into useless slivers.

Another man, followed by several more, burst into the restroom, took a quick look at the scene and said, "Pharaoh wept! What happen here, Rex?"

"This crip was suckin' Jimbo's johnson," Rex said, panting hard, "after Jimbo'd passed out drunk. Didn't think ol' Jimbo would've approved, you?"

"Shit, Rex, looks like you mighta killed the guy."

Blood was running out of both of Balzac Kicz's ears, as well as from his mouth and nose. His three-limbed body lay twisted in a posture best described as a figure-eight-minus-an-arc. Rex, who was rapidly regaining his composure, hawked and spat on the crumpled Kicz.

"Yeah, Buck, I reckon I mighta did," he said. "First faggot tonight. But hell, it's early yet."

Buck and the others laughed, then Rex said, "Best we get Jimbo into the fresh air. Gimme a hand."

Buck kicked Balzac's carcass aside and bent to it.

SNAKE HEADS

Dear Sugargirl.

Remember wen I rote you all that bout Mother Bizco mama name Virguenza bein blin an all an bein rape in St Louis cemetary well after this hapen to me wat Im gon tell you Mother an me hav a privat tak an she tell me it were not at all true jus a story she say giv strenth an hope to other yung womens. I bin wonder why somtim she tell difern storys bout hersef an she say it serv difren purpos. I gess she got the rite who am I say Mother Bizco ain rite all the good she do can be wrong. Yesterday we get 2 girls from China an I ask em they no Cris Chew but they don even spek english. Man who brot em to the Temple say they pay the snake heads in China lots of mony get em to Amerca by smuglin. Then they end up a slave in som factory or lik these girls was made into hos kep uptown som big ol house an only forteen yers ol. Snake heads wat they call the Chinamen send em over on ol leekey boats so meny sink in oshen. We gon keep the China girls les they be made go back to China by the govmen. Also I here som news bout Jimbo sombody takt him in a mens room of a bar but he OK. They fin the guy don it witout no head an one leg missin in Irish bayou but Jimbo tell the cops he don no wat happen in the firs place. I no Jimbo he don lie. Now the mos real rezon I rite you is I bout to hav a baby an I am hopin an prayin you be abel com to NO an be wit me do you think you can? This be very mos import to me Sug I hav a drem an God tak to me also the baby. I no this so hard to belev but it a boy his name Angel de la Cruz mean Angel of the cross. I so friten wen my hol body flot in air Mother Bizco say it a maculat consepshun but truth be the father a man sick in his min name Waldo Orchid. I lik to kill this man sam as the China girls lik to kill the snake heads. I no it a sin even think it but these men got som dises in they brane, snake head a good nam for em. I hop you be here soon I tell you the hol story. I pray you com Sug.

Love Baby

LAUGHTER iN THE DARK

Baby was standing in front of the A&P grocery on the corner
of Royal and St. Peter in the Quarter, about to pull up and
smoke a Kool from the pack she had just purchased inside the
store, when an old woman, half-bent at the waist, a casaba-
sized hump on her back covered by a purple shawl decorated
with gold letters of the Hebrew alphabet, came up and pressed
both of her gnarled hands to Baby's belly.

"Simon of Cyrene is risen," said the old woman. She lifted
her face and stared at Baby. The woman's eyes were clear
green, the eyes of a very young girl. Her irises sparkled like
yellow crystals.

"Say what?" asked Baby.

"Your child will be the second coming not of Jesus, but of
the angel who bore his cross. Black Simon the Cyrenian."

"How you know? Who you?"

The woman made the sign of the cross over Sister Esquerita's stomach, kissed the index and third fingers of her own
right hand, and touched them to the stunned sister's forehead.

The old lady smiled, displaying perfectly white, straight
teeth, and said, "Even the mystery which hath been hid from

ages and from generations, but now is made manifest to his saints."

"You a friend of Mother Bizco's?" asked Esquerita.

"I am the Mother of Harlots," she said, and turned away. Then the old woman looked back, and told Baby, "Watch for the sign in heaven, for you shall be taken to that great city which reigneth over the kings of the earth. And there shall be no night there, you will need no candle, neither light of the sun. For without are dogs, and sorcerers, and whoremongers, and murderers, and idolators, and whosoever loveth and maketh a lie. Thereafter shall ye live."

The woman walked off and Baby watched her cross over on Royal and continue to Pirate's Alley, where she turned right and disappeared.

A large, orange-skinned man, his face and arms covered with bright red spots, stood on an upside-down blue plastic milk box by the curb and announced: "The year was 1922. In the greatest football game of the era, Paul Robeson scored two touchdowns in a thirteen-to-nothing victory for the Milwaukee Badgers over Jim Thorpe's Oorang Indians, after which Robeson and Thorpe got into a terrible fight."

Baby dropped her Kools and began running on St. Peter Street, not stopping until she got to Burgundy. She leaned against the side of a building to catch her breath, then unexpectedly started to laugh.

"Ain't no use tryin' to figure out *nothin'*!" she said, and laughed some more.

SANCTUM

"Girl, am I glad to see you!" said Baby Cat-Face, embracing Sugargirl Crooks on the top step of the entrance to the temple.

"Look at you," said Sugar, double-eyeballing Baby's garb, a snow-white muumuu embroidered with dozens of tiny gold crosses. "Size of a house an' done up pure as Mother Theresa!"

"Ain' no mother yet. One mo' week, doctor say. Beside, dey calls me Sister aroun' here."

"Okay, Sister Baby, we gon' bring an angel into the worl', no doubt about dat!"

As Baby and Sugar were catching up on each other's news, Waldo Orchid sat in a green-banded lawn chair in his yard on Lapeyrouse Street. He wore only a triple-extra-large pair of chartreuse shorts, letting his enormous gut take the little sun New Orleans had to offer this mostly cloudy June afternoon. Waldo's mother, Malva, and his Tante Desuso had gone earlier to visit the tomb of his father, Tosco, at the graveyard of Holy Fantômes, today being the anniversary of Tosco's untimely death by rat. Visiting tombs was not Waldo's idea of getting a leg up on the morning, so he had declined his mother and aunt's invitation to join them. Gone be gone, the oversized Orchid believed. Life its ownself was tough enough to handle without tripping on tragedies passed by.

Waldo popped open the pull tab on a sixteen-ounce can of Pabst he had brought out to the yard with him, and drank half of it in one swallow. He sat still and listened to a trio of screeching blue jays argue, probably over a scrap of pork rind raided from the overflowing garbage cans by the side of the house. Waldo reminded himself that he had promised his mother to dispose of the waste. Later for that. The whole world is just like them jays, Waldo thought. What happened to Balzac Kicz, such as. Pitiful, way things go. That darkmeat toil in service of Mother Bizco, now she could make nasty nice and do it twice. But what come of it? Girl write a letter call me the devil. All I done she be party to. Could maybe made something fine with her, gone to Casino Magic a long weekend.

Six jets streaked overhead, vaporizing what was left of the sky. Waldo lifted the beer can to his lips, but just as he was about to finish off the Pabst, he felt a cold nudge on his right calf. He reached down to rub the spot without looking and froze at what felt like forty tenpenny nails simultaneously piercing his hand.

Waldo's scream was drowned under the residual thunder of jet engines. He turned and saw a six-foot-long alligator with its jaws clamped solidly below his right wrist. Waldo's attempt to pull away from the beast mostly succeeded. As he suddenly stood and stared at it, the leathery creature chunked twice on Waldo's severed hand before swallowing. When he looked at the bloody stump on his starboard limb, Waldo screamed again, and this time the noise was undisguised.

ANGEL BABY

"Push, Baby! Come on, girl," exhorted Sugar, "give it up for Angel!"

Baby gathered her strength, regained control of her breathing, and bore down hard.

"Here he come, darlin'!" Mother Bizco said. "Keep puffin'."

Angel de la Cruz did not slide so much as glide from Esquerita Reyna's womb. It seemed to Sugar, who had midwifed the birth with Mother Bizco, that the boy emerged with his arms outstretched, reaching for her or another. His color was as autumn leaves, red and gold, and he grabbed hold of one of Sugargirl Crooks's fingers and one of Mother Bizco's with either hand. He did not cry, but coughed and turned his heavy, slick, dark head toward the silver-blue light streaming from a window above Baby's bed.

"Fear not," intoned Mother Bizco, "for he shall be great in the sight of the Lord, and he shall be filled with the Holy Ghost."

"He that is mighty hath done to me great things," Baby panted. "Hand him to me."

Angel sought Esquerita's right breast and quickly suckled it.

"We know that we are of God, and the whole world lieth in wickedness," said Mother Bizco. "And we know that a son of God is come."

Angel quit Baby's tit, turned his slimy face toward Mother Bizco, and let loose a horrible sound, more moan than cry. He then fixed her with his eyes, both of which glowed briefly, but brilliantly, red. Mother Bizco sprang up and fell away from him as if pushed by a great wind.

Suddenly the window flew open, and a susurrant voice filled the room: "Wherefore didst thou marvel? I will reveal for thee the mystery of the woman, and of the beast that possessed her."

Mother Bizco crawled toward the infant and bowed her head, upon which he placed one of his surprisingly supple hands. Sugargirl noticed now that the fingers were webbed, and she began to weep. Baby, exhausted by the ordeal, and suddenly frightened, fainted into sleep.

NO RAiN iN eGYPT

"Best not distoib da boy, Malva. Let him catch his res'."

"But Desuso, he ain' ate since yesterday. Ain' like Waldo, you know dat. It rain in Egyp' before he refuse food."

"Boy been through a trauma, sister. I bring him some cream tomato soup later."

"Wit' saltine crackers."

"Yeah, sure. You think better to crumble 'em in da soup, or jus' put on da side?"

"Side be bes'. He want, we crumble 'em for 'im. He only got one hand now, crumble wit'."

At the thought of this, both women broke into tears and crossed themselves. Malva and Desuso had been tending to the wounded Waldo since his return the previous afternoon from Nuestra Perdita del Desierto Hospital. The doctors had cauterized his wrist and sewn it up. The animal control people had managed to extricate part of Waldo's hand from the gator's stomach after they had shot and killed it, but too little was left of the digits to attempt reattachment. Waldo would have to be fitted with an artificial hand or hook after the stump healed.

Loaded on Percodan, Waldo dozed in his room, his sanitarily dressed arm resting, slightly elevated, on a rubber pillow. He did not stir until an arrow passed through the fastened window next to his bed without breaking the glass and entered Waldo's open mouth. It penetrated the back of his skull, and lodged in the mahogany headboard decorated with a hideous oil painting purportedly depicting the Last Supper. Waldo gagged slightly upon impact, but that was all.

At the Temple of the Few Washed Pure by Her Blood, as the infant Angel de la Cruz was being baptized by Mother Bizco, there appeared on the ceiling above where the participants stood a holograph, the letters scorched in black across the white tiles:

AND THE LORD SHALL BE SEEN OVER THEM, AND
HIS ARROW SHALL GO FORTH AS THE LIGHTNING.

BEAUTIFUL PHANTOMS

At the age of one, on the evening of his birthday, Angel walked for the first time. Until that moment he had given no evidence of even the slightest interest in ambulatory activity. The boy was content to sit and observe his surroundings, seldom making an effort to crawl. Sugargirl Crooks had stayed on in New Orleans to take care of him since Sister Esquerita had become preoccupied with her interest in the invasion of the planet by extraterrestrials.

Baby was convinced that members of the religious right were not, in fact, human beings at all, but interplanetary travelers, invaders from some distant place in space. Mother Bizco asked Sugar to remain when she noticed the degree to which her Almost-Perfect acolyte seemed distracted. It was as if the process of pregnancy and birth had fundamentally undone the girl. Even Sugar had difficulty communicating with Baby, who would not talk at all to Mother Bizco or other members of the temple. Sugar realized a crisis stage had been reached when Baby refused to recognize Angel de la Cruz as her son.

For his part, Angel did not seem to mind his mother's inattentiveness. He ceased breast-feeding after two months, his teeth came in, and he ate whatever Sugar gave him. On the night that he began to walk, Angel also spoke his first words. Sugar was changing his diaper when he looked directly at her and said, "I will deliver thee out of the hand of the wicked, and I will redeem thee out of the hand of the terrible."

Sugargirl grabbed him up and ran to Mother Bizco, who was in the sacristy preparing a sermon, and told her what had occurred. Mother Bizco dropped to her knees, as did Sugar, and together they genuflected before the boy, who placed one of his hands on each of their heads.

"Receive ye the Holy Ghost," said Angel. "And do not be further concerned for my mother, for she dwelleth with beautiful phantoms."

As Angel comforted the women, Baby Cat-Face threw open the window in her room and climbed onto the sill. She stood stark naked, studying the dark sky. A radiant blue bridge appeared before her, leading from the window to a cloud. There came a bolt of bead lightning that rent the cloud, creating a door toward which Baby, fearless for the first time, began to walk.

THE LOST SONS OF CASSIOPEIA

MARKED FOR LIFE

"Pretty interestin', Angel, ain't it? Mean how you and me come to be cellmates after we both been busted at the same time on the same type beef, and got to serve the same amount of time."

"Only thing less interestin' than bein' alive, Sailor, is dead. That's a natural fact."

Angel de la Cruz Reyna and Sailor Ripley were inmates at the Pee Dee River Correctional Facility in North Carolina, where each man had been incarcerated for the crime of manslaughter. Sailor had killed a man named Bob Ray Lemon in a bar fight in his hometown of Bay St. Clement, after the man had aggressively and repeatedly insulted Sailor's girlfriend, Lula Fortune.

In a remarkably similar circumstance, Angel, who had come to Corinth, North Carolina, from New Orleans, to visit his cousin Gracielita Pureza, had encountered in a bar Gracielita's erstwhile boyfriend, a Montenegran-Gypsy immigrant named Romar Dart, confronted Dart about his physically abusive behavior toward Ms. Pureza, and then bested him in a Texas-style teardown, the result of which landed Angel a five-to-ten-mandatory two-year chill-out at Pee Dee and dealt Dart a permanent grounding of the literal persuasion.

Romar Dart had been working as a home-appliance salesman at Huge Huey's Discounteria. He was twenty-four years old, six months out of the army, in which service he'd done two consecutive stretches straight out of high school. Romar wasn't quite used to being a civilian, and he had a difficult time accepting the fact that Gracielita Pureza, who was only nineteen, could possess such an independent mind. Dart was emotionally adrift due to the loss of his parents in a car crash a fortnight before his discharge. Raimundo and Della Dart had been returning home from an evening of playing the slots at Poor Homer's Gates of Horn Casino, when a pig truck blew its left front tire and toppled across the white line onto Raimundo and Della's Lumina, crushing the elder Darts inside. Pigs spilled onto the road around the wreck, squealing and scrambling, causing motorists to swerve and stop suddenly, resulting in not a few whiplash cases, as well as several casualties of porcine nature.

Despite Gracielita's attempts at consolation, Romar could not shake the brutal feeling of having been abandoned by his parents. Gracielita put up with Dart's self-pity for a while, but finally told him to let it go and deal with the life ahead. Romar reacted violently, knocking her around his trailer and denting Gracielita's left temple with what had been Raimundo's favorite five iron. Angel de la Cruz had arrived in Corinth the day after this incident occurred.

Sailor lit a tailor-made and handed it to Angel, who took a drag and passed it back.

"We all of us lost sons of Cassiopeia, anyway," said Angel, leaning back on his bunk. "We marked for life."

"Sons o' who?"

"Cassiopeia, was an Ethiopian queen. This bitch was so vain, she claim she was better lookin' than the sea nymphs. That pissed off them bitches so much they commanded a sea serpent attack her daughter, the virgin Princess Andromeda, who the Oracle made her daddy, King Cepheus, chain to a rock in the water, so the serpent get at the girl."

"How you know all this?"

"Myths, man. You ain't read 'em?"

"No."

"Cat name Perseus rescue Andromeda. He the son of Jove, and a famous dragon slayer already had took out the Gorgon. So Perseus whips this sea monster, carves it up with his sword, and gets to marry the princess."

"Ethiopians is black, right?"

"Cassiopeia mostly was, I guess. Make Andromeda a quadroon, like my mama."

"What happen to her?"

"Cassiopeia? Or my mama?"

"No, Cassie, yeah."

"Oh, man, she be so mortify by the situation, trouble she cause, the word 'melancholy' be invented just describe her. After she die, Cassiopeia was sent to the stars because of her beauty, be the brightest light in her own constellation. But the sea nymphs still got the red ass about her and force the gods place Cassiopeia up top of heaven, near the pole, make her be humble by bendin' her neck."

"So what you mean by us bein' sons of her?"

"*Lost* sons. Mean we the kind of fools get too full of ourselves sometime, lose control. Look at us, man, where we are."

"You and me? Like in jail?"

"Not *like* in jail. *In* jail! We ain't paid nobody get here, have we?"

Sailor stabbed out the end of his cigarette on the wall and dropped the butt back into the pack for hard-ups.

"We just done what had to be done, Angel. What we had to do."

"And the man done what he had to do, too."

"You say your mama was what? Quadroon?"

"Right. One-quarter black. 'Bout like most the population of south Louisiana."

"And your daddy, what was he?"

"We don't talk about him."

"Assumin' he was white, what that make you?"

Angel's eyes turned red, blood spurted from the palms of his hands, and then he levitated, arms spread, feet together, floating until his back was flat against the ceiling of the cell. Sailor cringed on his bunk in disbelief, horrified, as he witnessed the blood dripping down from Angel's stigmata.

A voice filled the cell, saying, "The Son of man shall come in the glory of his Father with his angels."

Sailor watched the blood stain the floor. He tried to speak, to ask Angel what was happening, beg him to come down, but his mouth and throat were paralyzed. Angel's body began to spin, and Sailor collapsed, falling instantly into a deep sleep.

When he awoke, Sailor saw Angel standing by the cell door, leaning against it, smoking a cigarette.

Angel looked at him, held up the butt, and said, "Hope you don't mind, man. Stole one of yours."

"Hey, what's goin' on?" Sailor asked groggily. "I fell out, huh?"

Angel nodded. "Yeah, all of a sudden, like you been hit with a hammer."

Sailor shook his head. "Had a crazy dream, man. You were in it, too."

"What was I doin'?"

"Flyin', man. You were flyin' around the room, and there was blood everywhere."

Sailor looked down but there were no bloodstains.

"Blood?"

"Yeah, comin' off your hands."

Angel laughed and stamped his right foot.

"Hell, Sailor, that just sounds like Saturday night."

THE OTHER THING

Angel de la Cruz was taking his exercise in the main prison yard, lifting weights in the Pit with the crew of inmates who regularly worked out together. Oren Topo, a bespectacled, forty-six-year-old philatelist from Raleigh, who was doing a deuce-to-ten on an indecent exposure rap—revealing his private parts to a group of elementary school children during their morning recess—stumbled over a nearby barbell and fell on the ground directly in front of Angel as he released two hundred pounds of iron he had just clean and jerked. The portside weight bopped the top of Topo's head, causing his cranium to explode. Bone, flesh, and bloody fluids splattered the Pit, most of it sticking to Angel.

Edgar "One Big Dog" Grissom, the prison doctor, whose gigantic right foot earned him his nickname, took one quick look at the toppled Topo, then threw an eye to the sky, and said, "Surprised as shit the mushroom cloud ain't still hangin' in the air."

The question of the perverted philatelist's death being anything other than an accident was never raised; though there were those among the authorities who harbored a tiny thought about the possibility that Topo might have made an untoward suggestion to Angel to which the young man took exception. Nobody cared much about Topo, however; he had no family, and he was buried in the Pee Dee graveyard next to a former car thief from Rocky Mount named Tommy Dip. Dip had suffocated one night on his bunk when his cellmate, Igor Goose, stuffed six cotton socks down Dip's esophagus. Igor Goose, who never gave an explanation for his actions, had then blinded himself with a toothbrush and been sent to the H. D. Stanton Institute for the criminally insane.

Angel became severely depressed as a result of having caused Oren Topo's demise, accidental though it had been. He refused food for several days before finally accepting a plate of rice and red beans brought to him in their cell by Sailor Ripley.

"Good as hell to see you takin' sustenance again," Sailor told Angel. "Hate to see you ruin yourself over one crushed queer."

"Man is captain of his own salvation," Angel mumbled between mouthfuls, "made perfect through sufferings."

Sailor nodded and said, "Uh-huh. Better that than the other thing."

Angel finished off the plate, set it aside, and leaned back on his bunk.

"When I was a boy, I moved around a lot," he said. "Mostly to foster homes, and in between them the Jacob's Ladder Repository for Waifs of Color in New Orleans. What family I knew about, such as my cousins the Purezas, was too poor to claim me."

"My old man was a hard drinker," said Sailor. "Bein' home meant bein' beat."

"Least you had a home. Best one I had was with a woman in the Bywater run a funeral parlor. Her name was Thelma Mars. I was ten and a half years old then, and she treated me good. Would have stayed with Thelma Mars forever, but she lost her business license when they found Speedy."

"Speedy?"

"Yeah, Thelma Mars's ex-husband. Somebody turned her in to the embalmers union and they discovered his corpse, which Thelma Mars had embalmed herself forty years before. She kept Speedy dressed in a tuxedo, propped up in her bedroom closet. Authorities come and took the body away and entombed him in St. Louis Number Two."

"Did you know about, uh, Speedy?"

"Oh, sure. Mrs. Mars used to talk to him all the time. She liked me to sit in on the conversations sometimes."

"Conversations?"

"Yeah. She did the talkin' for 'em both, of course. I just listened."

"What would she—they—talk about?"

"The usual stuff. World events, the weather." Angel laughed. "Old Speedy had some strong-ass opinions, as I recall."

"Such as?"

"Thought guaco vine was the cure for cancer. He instructed Thelma Mars to make a guaco leaf paste and put it on our toast in the mornings."

"What's guaco?" asked Sailor.

"A tropical plant used as a remedy for snakebites. Speedy said if we ate guaco paste we wouldn't get cancer, which is what killed him."

"How'd it taste?"

Angel shook his head. "Can't remember, even though we ate the stuff every day for the six months I lived at the Absolute Truth Funeral Parlor. When the people from Jacob's Ladder come to take me back, Thelma Mars told me, 'Do not mourn for Speedy. He is a dead person, and there is no need to keep on keeping on. You don't cry over anything you have to give up, because you eventually must give up everything.' Words of wisdom."

"I guess so," said Sailor.

Angel smiled and said, "Daddy, it's the absolute truth."

KiSS OF THe NASONiA ViTRiPeNNiS

Angel de la Cruz was alone when he made his break. He had timed it carefully, making certain that the guard who patrolled the area near the sewage flow-thru pipe had just checked the culvert into which the prison waste emptied before beginning his furious crawl toward freedom. Angel knew his chance of success was far greater were he to go it solo, so he had not hinted of his plan to his cellmate, Sailor Ripley, or to any other inmate. Right now, as the population sat down for supper, there would be a minimum of latrine activity, and Angel seized the time, moving with alacrity.

The escapee slid down the final section of pipe into a horrific fecal swamp, attempting as best he could to keep intake of breath to a minimum. Angel knew if he stopped at all he would likely be overcome by methane fumes, so the lone progeny of what Mother Bizco had identified as an Immaculate Receptacle, Sister Esquerita Reyna, now part of an order beyond, let his seemingly winged feet do the talking.

He threw off his clothes on the riverbank and jumped into the water, desperate to rid his body of vileness. Angel swam downriver, ignoring the thick reptile presence he knew thrived in the writhing black moat. Moccasins kept their distance, however, repulsed by the demonic scent that Angel de la Cruz could never remove. At the third marker, he headed in, clambering up the muddy side into a tobacco field.

The ungodly child of shade fled naked down a crop row, the evening sky simmering sienna and gold and silent. No birds disturbed Angel de la Cruz's excruciating dash. When he saw the highway, he stopped and knelt next to the cancerous leaf, deciding in that instant to wait for nightfall before carrying out the remainder of his plan.

At total, moonless dark, Angel moved forward toward the road. He stood by the side of the two-lane and listened for a rumble, which sound did not impress his tympanic membrane until two or more hours had passed. As soon as Angel spotted the twin lights, he stepped out into the center of the highway, waving his arms in semaphore fashion.

The vehicle that bore down upon him was a late-model pickup truck of Japanese manufacture. It stopped before Angel and stood percolating in the still-intense heat left over from the too terribly long, infernal day. Baby's son swiftly took to the passenger side, opened the door, and jumped up into the cab. The driver was a woman of late middle-age.

"Evenin', ma'am," said Angel. "Hot, ain't it?"

"What isn't?" the woman said, and drove on.

After riding for a quarter of a mile in silence, Angel said, "I guess you're wonderin' why I don't have any clothes on."

"Naked came the stranger."

"My name is Angel de la Cruz Reyna, and I'm on the run from the Pee Dee River Correctional Facility."

"Jewel Wasp," answered the driver, extending the extraordinarily long, bony fingers of her right hand toward him.

Angel shook hands and, shocked at how cold hers was, quickly withdrew his own.

"Know all about it," she said. "I was sent to retrieve you."

Angel gripped the door handle and was about to bolt when the woman added, "Not by the law."

"Who by, then?"

"Friends of your mother's."

"My mother? She died when I was an infant."

"There's death, and then there's death."

"I don't understand."

"Allow me to explain. A jewel wasp is unremarkable to the naked eye, but seen through a lens of some magnitude, it's gorgeous. Its colors are iridescent and handle the light kaleidoscopically, reinventing angles. The female jewel wasp seeks out fly pupae and destroys them with her venom. She then deposits two- to four-dozen eggs in each puparium. The eggs hatch into larvae within two days and immediately commence devouring the feast provided by their mother."

"Why are you tellin' me all this?"

"Patience is a virtue, son. All too rare these days."

"Yes, ma'am."

"A couple of weeks later, adult wasps emerge. The males,

short-winged and incapable of flight, mate and expire in the patch of fly pupae in which they were born. The newly emerged, winged females fly away the moment the mating act has ceased, in search of fresh fodder."

At this point Jewel Wasp clasped Angel's penis in her right hand, holding it gently while she spoke.

"The female jewel wasp's great gift is her ability to control the sex of her offspring. After mating, she stores sperm in a singular organ, a spermatheca, which resembles a balloon. A thin tube is attached to one end, and attached to that tube is a muscle that either straightens out and allows sperm to pass to the egg, creating a daughter, or crimps the tube and blocks the sperm, allowing a son to be born."

Angel's cock had hardened considerably, and he did not discourage Jewel from stroking him with her cool fingers.

"The number of daughters produced depends on many factors, not least of which is whether she is the first wasp to lay eggs in that particular pupa. If she is, she'll lay mostly daughters; if she is second, more sons are made. In extremely rare cases, only one son is allowed to be born."

"I still don't get it," said Angel, finding it difficult, now that his cock was fully erect, to keep from squirming as the Wasp woman manipulated him.

Jewel pulled the truck to the side of the road and cut the engine. She released Angel's penis, pulled off her trousers, and in one extremely swift motion mounted him.

"You are living evidence of the exception to the rule," she said.

Jewel Wasp proceeded to take the overwhelmed man, inflicting stinging bites to his neck and head as she rapidly brought him to orgasm, extricating his seminal fluid seemingly without even the pretense of pleasure on her part. Upon completion of the act, Angel de la Cruz rested his head against the back of the seat and closed his eyes. Without dismounting, Jewel reached down under the seat with her right hand and came up with a Colt Python, the nose of which she pressed to Angel's lips.

"But the female reserves the right to revoke the life she granted," Wasp rasped.

Angel opened his eyes and his mouth at the same time, and Jewel jammed the barrel tip past his broken front teeth and partway down his throat before pinching the trigger.

PiT STOP

Jewel Wasp pulled her white Toyota half-ton into the rest area off I-55 near McComb, Mississippi, parked it, and got out. She stretched her five-foot-seven-inch, 140-pound body, shook it as would a wet dog who had bounded onto the porch after having been caught by a cloudburst. It was late afternoon of a cloudy day in mid-August, muggy and hot as it gets in the Magnolia State. She located the ladies' restroom and strode toward it, turning bill-backwards the teal Marlins ballcap she wore while driving to shade her pale green eyes. There were no other travelers visible, and a battered, blue two-year-old Thunderbird was the only vehicle beside Jewel's in the lot.

Jewel entered a stall, lowered her pants, positioned herself strategically over the toilet, and squatted slightly, urinating without sitting down. After that she rinsed her hands, face, and neck at a washstand. When she looked into the mirror above the basin she saw reflected in it two faces other than her own. Jewel did not immediately turn around, instead waiting for one or both of the men to speak before deciding on a plan of action.

"Heigh-ho, lady," said the skinnier and obviously older of the two. "Feelin' better now, are we?"

His high-pitched, screechy voice brought to Jewel Wasp's mind the sound of aluminum furniture being dragged across a patio.

"You fellas lost?" she answered, still watching them in the mirror.

The skinny one whinnied, grinned, and said, "Not at all. Looks like we're in the right place at exactly the right time. Don't you think, Parshal?"

The other man nodded, did not crack a smile, remained mum.

"Figure you got a fish, huh?" said Jewel.

Skinny stopped smiling, curled what would have been his upper lip had he had one, and said, " 'Bout to reel and deal, darlin'. You want it like that? In the butt? Watch both our cheeks twitch?"

The talker moved toward her, coming within a few inches before unbuckling and dropping his pants. He reached his long, thin, heavily veined arms around Jewel Wasp's waist, undid her trousers, and pushed them down.

"Well, well. Lady after my own heart, don't wear no panties."

Jewel felt the man's semierect penis push at her anus. The man grunted and bumped but his sex organ failed to fire sufficiently. No matter how furiously he rubbed and rocked, he could not summon an erection capable of penetrating her. The more he tried, the less responsive was his apparatus. Jewel did not make a move of her own volition.

"Shit!" he howled, and ripped the baseball hat from her head. "Damn!"

"Come on, C. J.," said the other man. "Let her be. It ain't gonna work, you know it."

C. J. kept pumping, but by now his penis was so limp that it just flapped against Jewel's buttocks. He stopped and stood there, panting hard.

"You do her then, Parshal," he said. "I'll hold her down, it's necessary."

"C. J., let's go. This is sick."

C. J. backed away from Jewel and hauled up his pants. He composed himself, brushed back his sparse red hair with both hands, held his nostrils closed one at a time, and blew snot on the floor from each.

"You're too old, lady," said C. J. "That's the problem. I'm go find myself a dainty young thing make my dick thick as a brick. No need to keep your sorry ass clean. Ancient! You're ancient, bitch! You hear me?"

The men left the restroom. Jewel stood in the same position, her hands gripping the sides of the washbasin. She heard glass breaking, then the roar of an automobile engine followed by the squeal of rubber on pavement. Slowly she relaxed her hands, flexed her fingers, then lifted and fastened her khakis. Jewel turned and searched the floor for her cap, which she located crown-up under the hand drier. She picked it up, put it on in the conventional manner, and walked outside.

The men—or, more likely, just the one called C. J.—had

busted out the front windshield of her truck. Jewel opened the driver's-side door, reached under the seat, and came up with her revolver. She walked back into the restroom and went over to the mirror in which the men's faces had appeared. Jewel lifted the Python, pointed it at the glass, and fired twice.

"Be vigilant," Jewel Wasp said aloud, "because your adversary the devil, as a roaring lion, walketh about, seeking whom she may devour."

BAD COMPANY

"Only one woman I ever truly love."

"Yeah? Who was dat?"

"You know."

"Oh, you means Baby Cat-Face."

"Uh-huh."

"Dat be forever ago, Jimbo. Forever ago."

"Seem like dis mornin'."

Jimbo Deal and Wig Hat Tippo, Jr., both men in their mid-sixties, sat next to one another on stools in the Evening in Seville Bar on Lesseps Street in New Orleans, drinking Ronrico cocktails. It was two o'clock on a Saturday afternoon in September. The temperature outside was ninety-five degrees Fahrenheit and inside, despite two creaking ceiling fans, only a touch cooler.

"Been what, Jim? Thirty years? What really happen I never did know."

Deal took a short sip, and said, "Girl got religious. Got wit da wrong comp'ny."

"Who, such as?"

"Mother Bizco and dem. Temple da Few Wash Pure by Her Blood. Drive Baby to suicide hersef."

"Oh, yeah. Shit, Jimbo, time peoples get a clue. Organize religion be dangerous to dey health. Ought to da gov'ment put warnin' signs on churches, same as on cigarettes."

Deal drained his glass, saw that Tippo's was half full, picked it up, and drained it, too.

"Life go on, Wig, you know? Ain' no place for it to go but on."

CODA:
LA CULEBRA

RUBY-BABY

Sidney Culatazo, the three-hundred-pound, sixty-five-year-old
night clerk at the Hotel La Culebra on Frenchmen Street in
the Marigny District of New Orleans, sat on a stool behind
the registration desk reading yesterday's *Times-Picayune*. Sidney
did not mind being a day behind on the news, he said, because by that time the current had disappeared from the
events; and besides, he reasoned, there was no way to know
what had really happened, anyway. Most so-called news was
the product of supposition and imagination, so what differ-
ence did it make when you read about it?

Chema Guapo, the eighteen-year-old handyman of La Culebra, came down the stairs carrying a mop and bucket.

"If dis don't crack da nut," said Sidney. "Lissen up."

Chema stopped at the foot of the stairs and waited.

"A would-be thief, some cockamamy *ladrón*, came to a sticky
end when he began sniffin' da glue he was stealin' from a
shop in da Brazilian city of Belo Horizonte. Overcome by da
fumes, da man collapsed, upsettin' a tank o' glue an' stickin'
his self to da floor da shop. He lay there for thirty-six hours,
unable to tear his self free, before firemen managed to cut

him loose. Jesus wept! Da kid couldn't even wait to get da shit out da door."

"Why you say it's a kid?" said Chema. "It say in the paper was a kid?"

"Couldn't be no grown man be dis dumb. Had to be was a kid."

"Plenty kids I heard in Brazil got no home, sleepin' in the street. Cops murder 'em, ain't nobody care."

"Bet any one dem Brazilian street arabs be grateful as hell have your job, hey, Chema? Don't you think? Mop up a bathroom, move a board, stop a leaky roof. Work for half wages, I bet."

"Yeah, maybe. Then one morning you wake up with a big grin on your fat neck. Look up see the devil pokin' at you with his pitchfork, sayin', 'Get to work, old man.' "

"No question you can't trust kids dese days."

"Even me?"

"Even you. Cousin Lester calmed down now?"

"He ain't never calm and still can't piss straight. Why is it you old men can't piss straight? Piss left, right, on your shoes. Every place but in the toilet. Oughta just sit down like a woman, take a piss."

"You got a better job lined up, hey?"

"Don't want one. I'm in love with moppin' up after old guys their dicks bend wrong."

Chema walked out of the hotel into Frenchmen Street to wring out his mop and dump dirty water. Sidney Culatazo reached down and picked up a small boa constrictor, which wrapped itself around his arm.

"You need a pet from Daddy?" Sidney cooed to the reptile. "You don't talk ugly like that sick boy, do you? No, no, no."

A young woman entered the hotel, dragging a steamer trunk along the floor. She was dressed Hollywood cowgirl style, her platinum hair long and loose over her face. She dragged the trunk into the middle of the lobby, sat down on it, and lit a cigarette.

"I'm lookin' for a room won't strangle my dreams," she announced. "A room'll let the dreams live in it. Don't tell me I'm talkin' shit, mister. I know how rooms work and I got to come to terms with these dreams. You got somethin' you can show me?"

Sidney looked her over, guessed her age at no more than twenty-one, and said, "Da question is, how much room your dreams take up?"

"Too much, sometimes. Others, not nearly enough."

"I discourage dreams myself," said Sidney. "I mean, personally. Used to dey would get in da way of what I needed or wanted to be thinkin' about, so I don't have 'em no more."

"Not that I'd want to, of course," said the young woman, "but how'd you stop 'em?"

The obese night clerk laughed. "New York would pay big money to know dat, sister. You come in on da red wind an' jus' aks, an' I'm suppose' hand out da secret. What's your name?"

"Ruby-Baby Wasp. Please, mister, I'm tired now. A room with any kind of window would do."

"Who's payin'?"

Ruby-Baby Wasp went over to the desk, dug a roll of bills out of her jeans, and put it on the counter.

"Cash ain't never been my problem," she said.

Sidney picked out a fifty, then banged a fat fist on the bell in front of him.

"Chema!" he shouted.

Chema came back in from the street and put down his mop and pail.

"Show Miz Wasp to twenty-one," said Sidney.

"That's next to Cousin Lester," Chema said.

"I know where it is."

Chema took the room key from Sidney, stuck it between his teeth, then lifted one end of the steamer trunk and began dragging it away.

"You'll let me know, it's okay," Sidney addressed Ruby-Baby's back.

Without turning around, she answered, "Shy is what a horse does," and followed Chema up the stairs.

Marisa Sopapo, the hotel maid and house prostitute, staggered in the front door, her hair awry, her orange poorboy barely containing her late-adolescent pulchritude.

"Am I late?" she asked Sidney.

"Cousin Lester's been waitin' on you. Better get up there."

She headed for the stairs.

"I know I'm a lucky girl," Marisa said, "you ain't got to tell me."

Cousin Lester, a carrot-topped, freckle-faced, skinny man in his late forties, lay on the bed in his small room reading the 1947 edition of Richard von Krafft-Ebing's *Psychopathia Sexualis*. This was Cousin Lester's favorite book, and he had read part of it every day for fifteen years. Today he was re-examining Case 31, that of patient J. H., aged twenty-six, who in 1883 consulted Krafft-Ebing concerning severe neurasthenia and hypochondria. Cousin, which was his given name, lived in the city of books. His room was filled with them, piled from floor to ceiling, even over the one window. Indian trail paths led from door to bed to washbasin to water closet to a table with a hot plate on it. He cared little for company, and read aloud to himself, as he did now.

" 'Patient confessed that he had practiced onanism since his fourteenth year, infrequently up to his eighteenth year, but since that time he had been unable to resist the impulse. Up to that time he had no opportunity to approach females, for he had been anxiously cared for and never left alone on account of being an invalid. He had no real desire for this unknown pleasure, but he accidentally learned what it was when one of his mother's maids cut her hand severely on a pane of glass, which she had broken while washing windows. While helping to stop the bleeding he could not keep from sucking up the blood that flowed from the wound, and in this act he experienced extreme erotic excitement, with complete orgasm and ejaculation.

" 'From that time on,' " Cousin Lester read, " 'he sought in every possible way to see and, where practicable, to taste the fresh blood of females. That of young girls was preferred by him. He spared no pains or expense to obtain this pleasure.' "

There was a knock at Cousin Lester's door.

"Hypotenuse!" he shouted.

Marisa Sopapo, who had knocked, shouted from the hallway, "The side of a right-angled triangle that's opposite the right angle!"

"*Bienvenida!*" said Cousin Lester.

Marisa entered the unlocked room and threaded her way through the ceilingscrapers of books to the bed, where she sat down next to Cousin Lester.

"An imaginary being inhabiting the air," she said.

"A sylph!"

Cousin Lester dropped Krafft-Ebing and embraced Marisa. She reached over and pulled the chain on his lavender-shaded china sailfish bedside lamp, extinguishing the light.

In the room next door, Ruby-Baby Wasp opened her trunk. She removed from it the well-thumbed, thick, red-covered notebook in which her mother, Jewel Wasp, had written her feminist opus, *Great Women I Have Heard about But Never Met*. Jewel Wasp had died while giving birth to Ruby-Baby, her only child, and Ruby-Baby had been raised by African-American nuns of the Order of Simone the Cyrenian at Miss Napoleon's Paradise for the Lord's Disturbed Daughters in Oktibbeha County, Mississippi, the institution where Jewel Wasp was confined at the end of her life.

Ruby-Baby often turned to her mother's unpublished book when she was at an impasse with her dreams. The chapter Ruby-Baby Wasp resorted to most often was the one about Sister Esquerita Reyna, an acolyte of Mother Bizco's legendary Temple of the Few Washed Pure by Her Blood, known to many by her secular name, Baby Cat-Face. Ruby-Baby believed she was Baby's namesake.

In her book, Jewel Wasp claimed to have conceived a child with Sister Esquerita's son, Angel de la Cruz, the issue being Ruby-Baby, whose name she wrote down before giving birth. Upon her departure from the Paradise at the age of eighteen, the nuns of the Order of Simone the Cyrenian had given Ruby-Baby her mother's manuscript, but warned her that, in their opinion, much, if not all, of the information contained therein was specious. About Ruby-Baby's paternity, of course, there could be no certainty. All that she knew for a fact about her mother was that Jewel had been suspected of having murdered in cold blood more than fifty men, including Angel de la Cruz Reyna, prior to her commitment to Miss Napoleon's Paradise for the Lord's Disturbed Daughters.

As Ruby-Baby Wasp perused her legacy, she was disturbed by bestial sounds of lovemaking that penetrated the thin wall between her room and Cousin Lester's. The wild noises only deepened Ruby-Baby Wasp's despair over what she perceived as the endless nightmare of sex and death. The last sentence in her mother's book haunted Ruby-Baby, and she turned to it now. "In my distress I cried unto the Lord," Jewel had written, "and *He did not listen!*" Those four, final words, Ruby-Baby believed, had been underlined by Jewel Wasp with her own blood.

THE UNSPOKEN

Cousin Lester's people hailed from rural Winston County, Alabama, the place of his own birth. He had been raised, however, in Birmingham. His mother, Louise Elizabeth Lovely, called Lou-Liz, claimed never to have seen a black person until she was twenty-one years old and newly arrived in the city of Birmingham. His father, Perno Holgado Lester, moved with his wife and two-year-old son to the big town to work as a roofing contractor. The building trades were booming at the time in Birmingham, enabling Perno to provide decently for his family. Lou-Liz, who always had been an avid reader, a book-club member from the age of eleven, obtained part-time employment at a branch library, and inculcated in Cousin what became an enduring love of literature and quest for knowledge.

Perno Lester had been a big believer in life insurance, and when he and Lou-Liz were killed in an airplane crash on what was both their first and their final flight—Birmingham to Miami, where they were to connect with a junket to the Bahamas for the first vacation of their lives—Cousin, who was twenty-two at the time, became the sole beneficiary of a sizable sum of money. Cousin used this inheritance conservatively, investing it mostly in utilities, which paid him regular dividends. He had managed never to work, the tragedy-engendered windfall having come the day following his graduation with a degree in Library Science from the University of Alabama.

New Orleans suited Cousin Lester better than Birmingham or Tuscaloosa. He enjoyed the variegated population, and it was a good book town. His real desire was to write, and it was Marisa Sopapo who inspired him in this endeavor. She was the first woman, he felt, who truly shared his vision of the world, despite her lack of formal education and her modest standing in society. When his first piece of creative prose appeared in a local literary magazine called *The François Villon Review*, Cousin dedicated it "To Marisa, my Muse." Marisa thanked Cousin Lester for this, responding in kind by throwing him a freebie, but admitted to Sidney Culatazo that she had never even attempted to read it. In fact, Marisa confessed, she could not read, though she could remember and repeat verbatim virtually anything she had ever heard.

The Unspoken
by Cousin Lester

1

I begin like any other man, without a plan. I am staying in a seaside resort, one of many, in no particular country; perhaps somewhere on the Ionian Sea. Yes, I recall the insignificant waves, waves hardly to be disturbed by. There is a beach, of course, though I avoid sand; it reminds me so painfully of the deserts of my childhood. The many flowers are in bloom but I can never remember the names of flowers or plants other than bougainvillea, which grows everywhere around the town. For these flowers to thrive the weather must remain hot for several months, which it does. It is very hot every day, each day of my residence.

I was born without a mouth. Can you believe this? I am forty-eight years old, I have been living for almost a half century with this condition, an extraordinary circumstance, and yet still I find this situation incomprehensible. It is also ridiculous not to have a mouth. Think of it—of course, you already have—to be unable to talk or eat in a conventional manner. One never grows used to this handicap. At least, I have not.

The absence of a mouth—my mouth, the one intended for me (I have always believed that God intended to give me a mouth; this belief is unshakable)—has no bearing on this story. An adventure has a life of its own and my life, the life of a natural freak, is irrelevant here (other than as a terrible detail that I implore you to ignore). I do not even know or understand why I mention it. (Perhaps being without a mouth, the idea of this crime obsesses me and will lead to an unfortunate circumstance. We shall see.)

Did I mention that I am alone in this seaside village? I am isolated if not alone in the strictest sense of the term. By definition a person has no choice in the matter. (Or have you, the reader, chosen not to question whichever myth with which you have been informed? It doesn't matter, it really doesn't. Believe me.) There are no birds on the island. (Is it an island? I can't remember.) This is an amazing fact, a stupendous piece of illogic. Consider you are at the seaside and are expecting, as you should be, to see birds, a flock of them, at least a single frigate or tern or gull, and after two days you experience the terrible realization that no birds *exist*. This is what happened to me. (I would have asked someone, a fellow guest at the hotel where I am staying, but of course, as you now know and cannot forget—I won't let you, you can be certain—I had no mouth with which to do so. Being supremely unlike any other person has its disadvantages, as well as advantages an ordinary individual could not begin to imagine.)

The absence of birds notwithstanding, I decided to stay. I will not keep you in suspense any longer (Why should I, a man without a motive, or a mouth?)—the reason I fled the city (a large one, named R.), exchanged it like a soiled glove (I am very fond of gloves) for the featherless seaside resort town (I will call it T.), had to do with a woman. She rejected me, after several years of friendship. I must bite my tongue (figuratively speaking—but then, neither am I able to speak) as I write that. If you have read this far in my narrative, you are not readily or easily fooled. Forgive me for not being entirely honest at the outset. (I feel more ridiculous asking for forgiveness than I do upon entering a public place where nobody knows me and they stare at the area of my face below the nose where a mouth, any kind of mouth—even a narrow one, with thin lips—should, by all God intended, be.) F. and I had been lovers for four years. This fact is inescapable. I must admit that it gives me pleasure (a pleasure of sorts, I suppose) to say this. Is it incomprehensible to you that a woman as beautiful (I believe she is beautiful) and intelligent (this, too, though remember I am easily fooled) as F. should have accepted for her lover a man without a certain feature? Of course, had she not been an extraordinary person to begin with I could not have loved her. I still love her. Though we are no longer together, it does not mean that my powerful feeling for F. has ceased to exist. I am essentially an honest man.

2

I had, as I say, no plan when I arrived at T. I had never even considered going to T., had never heard of the place before my last-minute departure. No, that is not entirely true; I had heard of T. When I was a boy, our housekeeper, M., used to mention the place now and again. I believe she had some relatives there that she would visit on occasion. M. had beautiful feet. I first saw them when I crawled around the house, before I could walk, and M. would do her chores barefoot. Her feet were extraordinarily long and slender, like ferrets. It was painful for me when my parents fired M. for stealing. I was then seven years old. I thought that M. would return sometime, but she never did. Luckily, I have no problem conjuring up images of her perfect heels, delicate arches, and exquisite toes. F.'s feet are much smaller, her toes bent in various directions, tortured worms. I cannot consider them in the same category with those of M., the angelic housekeeper of my youth.

The subject, the suggestion of T., of my going there, presented itself late one night as I was riding in a taxi. It had been raining all that day and into the evening. The streets and buildings of the city in which I live were blackened by water. The entire city resembled a discarded tire floating in the sea. For a moment the downpour abated, and when the taxi froze suddenly at a stoplight I could see through the glass a poster hanging in a shop window advertising T. Just as suddenly, the taxi sped forward again, forcing the issue; it would be necessary for me to investigate the possibility of T.

It is important for me to accept that F. found a morbid self-image in my anatomical anomaly. (How many ways, after all, is it possible to say "without a mouth"?) I believe absolutely that she enjoyed becoming involved with my predicament. Whether this intrigue included a particular sexual component on her part I (naturally) cannot say. F.'s fondness for brushing her lips along that area of my face below my nose and above my chin I did not attribute to any bizarre fascination. After all, other than with their genitals, this is the most natural place for lovers to combine. Sympathy for her arose in me, however, when I realized how often she yearned to be kissed (though she never spoke of it). Regardless of our repeated coupling, a sense of something missing progressively became an overwhelming factor in our relationship.

A surgical remedy was out of the question. As a child, I was subjected to numerous medical examinations. Due to an unusual (What is not unusual in this case?) configuration of blood vessels in what should have been my orthodontal region, the specialists deemed invasive measures too precarious for purposes of plastic reconstruction.

The first question, of course, is always: How do you eat? In ancient times, I would have been slaughtered at birth. At first sight, upon expulsion from my mother's womb, the hideous creature—I—would certainly have had the briefest of sojourns on this earth. It is believed that a baby does not exercise its vision for two or three weeks, in which case never would I have been able to experience sight, my greatest pleasure. The question of sustenance never would have been raised. As it is, in this most medically aggressive age, intravenous feeding has become almost de rigueur. I possess all relevant bodily functions; several times a day, at my convenience, I am sustained via injection. At the age of three, desiring to emulate my playmates, I attempted to ingest regular food—carrots, I believe—through my nostrils. I succeeded only in very nearly asphyxiating myself. This terrible lesson served me well. I knew then, barely beyond infancy, that I controlled death. Subsequently, of course, I learned of the infinite ways in which death controlled me, and that I was an amateur in this department, a novice for whom sophistication would remain a hopeless fantasy.

3

If nobody had a mouth then who would inhabit the lie? How would it be verbalized? How could any condition beyond death go unrecognized? F., being beyond life—my life, for now (or forever)—is also beyond death. She has no choice but to exist forever (for now) at variance with the universe as I perceive it. Perception is not properly open to competition. Opinions are replaced repeatedly and with increasing facility. Nothing can prevent this.

It was not F.'s way to directly reprimand me; never would she act so overtly. Unpleasant circumstances provoked her to laughter, a response which she herself found baffling. This enigmatic mirth, I informed F., was a not uncommon nervous reaction; an obviously involuntary seizure belying no especial significance. F., however, believed her behavior at such moments to be most unseemly; nothing I could say could disabuse her of this opinion.

F., then, for the sake of this story, which is, of course, not a story. (I never really intended it to be.) If I say she is tall and dark, or fragile, just that, it conveys so very little. There is a darkness in her that she struggles to avoid; it eats at her like a rash on the inside of her skin. The way she moves expresses inexorable distress. Often her movements are those of a lizard on a terrace in the hot sun. She skitters, stops, jerks her head, flaps her eyelids (Do lizards have eyelids? If not, why not?), runs on, light evaporating the colors on her spine: green and blue become gray. F. is serious as she pretends to gaiety. This attitude frightens and—I must confess—delights me. Her vulnerability shrieks at the sky.

I adore F. and do not blame her for her defection. A predicament such as mine is not nullifying, not in any sense expressive of finality. At least it does not impress me in this way. F., on the other hand, has imposed upon herself a philosophy so restrictive in its parameters that there is virtually no opportunity for her to entirely relax. I do not refer particularly to her impatience with me. How would it be possible for a person—any person of even adequate intelligence and perceptivity—not to be occasionally intolerant?

It is quite common for people to convulse in the presence of a freak. Even F. has become overwhelmed at the sight of me, despite our long association. She will begin to think of me as being entirely normal in appearance, then suddenly turn to speak to me and be shocked at what she sees. The fear in her eyes when this occurs is unmistakable. Her heart palpitates, her throat and mouth dry up, she stutters when she attempts to regain her faculties. I must remain calm at such moments, endure these seizures of naivete without a flinch of self-hatred.

I do not loathe myself, after all; it is everyone else whom I loathe. Others have not the complete privilege of seeing how disgustingly weak they are. Confrontation connotes nausea, and this incautious behavior precludes the possibilities of seriousness.

(Reprinted from *The François Villon Review*, Vol. 1, No. 2)

THE BIG RED SPOT

"I ever tell you how my mama died?" Marisa Sopapo asked Cousin Lester.

"No, tell me."

Cousin Lester was sitting up in bed reading *The Aerodynamics of Vortiginous Levitation*. Marisa, lying next to him, smoked a cigarette as she spoke.

"Hoodoo spirit took possession over her body, rode her like it was the Kentucky Derby, until my Grandmama Hypolite Cortez cut off her head."

Cousin Lester dropped his book and said, "Your grandmother beheaded her own daughter?"

"Yeah. Spooky, ain't it? A demon had saddled itself on Mama's shoulders, made her act crazy. Mama poked out both her own eyes first, but the spirit still wouldn't let go."

"Poked out her eyes?"

"Blind horse can't see where it's goin', so usually that'll cut loose the rider. For some reason, Mama couldn't shake what had hold of her, so Grandmama made sure Mama's sufferin' would end."

"Kind of a drastic solution," said Cousin Lester. "Why'd this demon possess your mama in the first place?"

"Someone hexed her for stealin' away a man. Woman named Imogene Moutard, was furious about Mama carryin' on with Billy Egypt, Imogene Moutard's ex. She still had the hots for him. Went to a hoodoo lady up in Arcadia, got a spell put on Mama."

"What happened to your grandmother?"

"She got charged with unlawful decapitation, but died about a month after from kidney disease. Didn't want to be plugged into no machine."

"That's a sad story, Marisa."

"I guess. Fella from up East—New York, I think—heard about it. He came down and interviewed me for a book he was writin' called *The Big Red Spot*. Bought me a mess of drinks at Duck's Colorado Club."

Cousin Lester leaned over and kissed Marisa on the forehead.

"God didn't intend the planet to be such a terrible place," he said.

Marisa put out her cigarette against the wall above her head. Her eyes teared up and she asked, "Then why the hell he make so many bad people?"

POSTCARD

Dear Ruby-Baby I get your letter yesterday
and I please to reply. People is so nasty
to each other cause of Fear. They opres
humilat hord divide and destroy in order to
Create Hell wich is nothin. The fearfull
and unbeliever the abominable the murderers
sorcerers idol worship and all Liars doom
theyself to the second Death wich is Life.
Baby Cat Face feel no Pain she blissfull in
Death. It a condishin so close resemble
Life that it sure surprise her since she
expec a band of angels hangin in the cloud.
She think estrateristils entise her take
that Fatefull Step in another dimenshin but
when the Veil of Sadness was raise to
Reveal a Face with wich she long be familar
but never seen Baby understan the Purpose
of Being. I an old lady now girl but I got
my mind Right.

Claudette Crooks

Ruby-Baby Wasp
Hotel La Culebra
Frenchmen Street
New Orleans, Louisiana

BARRY GIFFORD was born on October 18, 1946, in Chicago, Illinois, and raised there and in Key West and Tampa, Florida. He has received awards from PEN, the National Endowment for the Arts, the Art Directors Club of New York, and the American Library Association. His writing has appeared in *Punch*, *Esquire*, *Cosmopolitan*, *Rolling Stone*, *Sport*, the *New York Times*, the *New York Times Book Review*, and many other publications. Mr. Gifford's books have been translated into fifteen languages, and his novel *Wild at Heart* was made into an award-winning film. His book *Night People* was awarded the Premio Brancati, the Italian national book award established by Pier Paolo Pasolini and Alberto Moravia. He lives in the San Francisco Bay area.

The text of this book was set in Joanna, a typeface designed by the eminently eccentric English artist Eric Gill (1882–1940). It is a face of spartan simplicity—"a face free from all fancy business," as Gill himself described it—with an attractive, slightly quirky elegance.

Designed by David Blankenship